RESTORING
HEZEKIAH

RESTORING

HEZEKIAH

REVISED EDITION
AN AUTOBIOGRAPHICAL NARRATIVE
by
Hezekiah Morris

CHANGING A GENERATION

Www. AuthorDNMiller.Com

Authordnmiller@gmail.com

Pittsburgh, Pa
August 16, 2020

Library of Congress Control Number: 2017932158
Print information available on the last page.

Morris, Hezekiah.
Restoring Hezekiah (Changing a Generation)

P.CM. in Library of Congress Cataloging-in-Public Data

ISBN 978-1-7349511-4-1

Cover design by DN Miller Publications & Services

This is a work of creative nonfiction. The events are portrayed to the best of Hezekiah Morris's memory. While all the stories in this book are true, some names and identifying details have been changed to protect the privacy of the people involved.

DN Miller Publications & Services helps with self-publishing.

DEDICATION

I have dedicated this book to the loving memory of my gracious grandmother, Janie Morris. She instilled in me a sense of hope and blessings, as I pursue my dream of a transformed life.

I have also shared this dedication with Sherica Lanette, my loving significant other, and my precious loving daughter, Kyla Israel. Thank you for believing that the best of Hezekiah Morris was yet to come! You loved yourselves enough to love me so that we can mutually live out our dreams. Whether you know it or not, you gave me determination, and for that, I am eternally grateful.

GLORY TO THE LORD FOR GIVING ME LIFE, HEALTH, AND STRENGTH TO BECOME A BETTER MAN!

Restoring Hezekiah

By Hezekiah Morris
Revised edition

CONTENTS

ACKNOWLEDGEMENTS

I've had a rough life, but thank God through Jesus Christ for giving me a new life! Therefore, I would like to thank Him first for bringing me into the *glorious liberty* of the children of God!

I was a chief sinner. Christ changed my life from the inside out, and for that, I am eternally grateful. *"Come now, let us settle the matter,' says the Lord. Though your sins are like scarlet, they shall be white as snow; though they are red like crimson, they shall be as wool"* (Isaiah 1:18).

I would like to express my sincere thanks to my daughter's mother, Eve. Thank you for raising our child with love and care and knowing that loving her is more important than disliking one another. You are an inspiration and an example of motherhood today. Thank you for your support and for that I will love you forever.

To my daughter, Kyla Israel ("Bootie"), I love you very much. God's *agape* love helps me to love you unconditionally. Although I may have failed many times before, I want you to know that this is a new day. With Christ in my life, I have become a better man and hope to make a difference in your future. You have a beautiful life before you, and there is no limit to what you can do through faith in Christ. I cannot change the past, but we all can make a difference today and tomorrow.

To "Preacher man," thanks for helping me make it this far along my new life journey. You are an instrument and vessel that God used to give me a new direction in life. Your coaching and counsel, patient guidance, and prayers were and still are an inspiration to me.

To Mrs. Paulette, I am speechless because you have done so much for me. Thank you a thousand times over for

11

all your help and encouragement. You are an example of what the Bible means when it says to *love your neighbor as you would love yourself*. The virtues of God's peace, blessings and happiness flow from you and may they return to you and your family twofold.

When I was in jail, my cellmate "Pooh" was a tremendous inspiration to write my book. Thank you for tolerating me and listening to my story. Keith ("Ke-ka") was also an inspiration and motivator to write my story. The Lord willing, the next book will be a co-authored book written by him and me.

Mr. T ("Trouble"), thank you for giving me the idea for this book. Although you gave me a different title, the idea stayed the same. If God allows me to write a second edition, that will be the name.

To Officer A.R. Henderson, thank you for your support. Your encouraging words moved me forward. Mr. Drummond, thank you for letting me know the goodness of God. Your prayers reached up to heaven, came back, and resonated in my heart, which gave me strength.

I would like to thank my best friend, Aaron Rosser, for his loyalty and companionship over the years. I appreciate your friendship through our difficulties.

To Bishop Morris, I can never repay you for all that you have taught me over the years. You and "Momma Mollie" are a gift from God.

Thanks to you Grandma Morris. I know heaven is a better place because you are up there. Save a seat for me, because I will see you again one day. I hope you are looking down on me and feel proud of how I have changed. To my father, mother, and my brother, I love you. Thank you all because you have inspired *Restoring Hezekiah*.

I saved the best for last. Special thanks to my lovely fiancée, Sherica. I love you more than words can express. Thank you for believing in me when others may have doubted and for

12

pushing me when I wanted to give up on my dreams. You are my rock, my backbone, and everything to me.

INTRO

THE BEAST

Some things in life we quickly forget. We forget them because they were not significant events. Some non-traumatic things that happen in our lives, we dismiss from memory because they were not painful and did not leave a scar on our hearts. However, there are those painful, traumatic events that scar us for life. We try to bury those memories deep in our conscience, but other things that happen later in life bring those memories back, and they still hurt. **This story is about the pain of my past that affected my future.**

***

Thirty-seven years ago, it was a cold winter morning in my city where I was born. There was a light dusting of snow on the ground, which made Christmas feel more like Christmas. A chilly wind was blowing, but the snow and wind did not dampen the fire of Christmas in my heart. That is until the *Beast* walked in!

It was 1:30 am Christmas morning. I was in my formative years as a child, but I remember the events of that day as if it was yesterday. My younger brother, Joseph, as usual, was with me as we expected Santa's arrival. As kids growing up in our household, you could barely sleep anticipating what we thought Santa would bring.

In the living room, our beautiful Christmas tree that we helped to decorate was blinking brightly with an array of colors. My brother and I snuck out of our bedroom to keep mom from seeing us. We peeked down the hall from our bedroom door to make sure that the coast was clear. We cautiously made our way down the hall to the blinking tree. When we reached our destination, we started quietly opening our gifts. We were ecstatic as we whispered to each other!

Suddenly the front door knob began twisting and turning as if someone was attempting to break into our home. It startled us, so we looked up with eyes wide open and stopped opening our presents. Strangely, whoever was at the door on the other side inserted a key into the key lock. Who could it be? My young mind thought it was Santa, as I exclaimed that it was Santa to my brother.

My brother and I looked at each other with wonder. First, we thought about running and hiding, and then we said, *"What the heck,"* it's Christmas, what could go wrong. Besides, the turning and twisting of the doorknob stopped.

We continued opening our gifts, then suddenly the front door swung open wide as if someone forced it open. What stood before us scared the living hell out of us. It was a Beast!

The Beast's speech slurred as he yelled out profanity at my brother and me. He was rocking and reeling, swaying back and forth like a big bear looking for prey. His red eyes beamed with vicious rage and frightened us even more as he stared my brother and me down.

Because we had seen something like this before, suddenly our fear left. Could it be the same as what we experienced before? My brother looked at me and said, *"It's him, he's back."* We were not afraid anymore because we had seen this Beast many times before.

The Beast then opened his mouth and roared like a raging lion, *"Get your asses back to bed now!"* We frantically jumped up and ran back to our rooms. We left our bedroom doors slightly open, so we could listen to the Beast prowl through the house. We wanted to know where he was just in case we needed to run.

The Beast stumbled carelessly, like a drunken man, down the hall bouncing from wall to wall until he made it to his habitat, where our mother was waiting. Our mother spoke to the Beast in a stern voice and said,

"Them kids could have stayed up; it is Christmas. You should have left them alone. It don't make no sense."

The Beast roared back,

"Shut the hell up!"

Then the Beast lashed out at our mother, and with his claw-like hand smacked her across her face and told her to, *"shut up"* again. He didn't stop there. The Beast began choking her with a death-like grip and hitting her repeatedly with more force until she was non-resistant. Then he demanded that she have sex with him.

***

My brother and I watched from our bedroom. We wanted to help, but we were scared for our life because of what the Beast would do to us. Anger was now building up as tears welled up in our eyes.

This was a typical scene, just a little worse than others. We had come to it see all too often, so we knew it would pass. Five minutes later the house was quiet as a mouse and the Beast, my father fell asleep in a drunken stupor. Then my brother and I went back to opening our gifts as if nothing ever happened.

***

17

This is only one of the many horror scenes that took place in my childhood that lead to the man that I was and the man I have become today.

Remembering those things brings to my mind the code of silence that existed then. It was like an old wife's tale that the woman was to be "seen and not heard." The adage was like the slogan from Vegas. "What goes on in your house stays in the house." They would forbid us to speak about the abuses and the domestic violence that happened in the home. However, to get free from the trauma of ones' past, we must be willing to talk about what took place in our lives — the good, the bad, and the ugly. Communication helps to vent the pain of the past. Today, it is time to break the silence and tell my story.

What happened to me? What kind of man did I become? Join the journey and discover the truth! Let's get started. What does *Restoring Hezekiah* mean through my life journey?

CHAPTER 1

FOR MY NAMESAKE

Hezekiah was a real King in the dynasty of the nation of Israel. He was the thirteenth King of the Southern Kingdom; Judah after the Kingdom of Israel divided into the north and south Tribes. He was a good king and did right in the sight of the Lord. His name in the Hebrew means *God is my strength*, or *God has strengthened*.

Some sources say that people with the name Hezekiah have a deep inner desire for love and companionship, and want to work with others to achieve peace and harmony.

I am not into astrology, but people with that name tend to initiate events, to be leaders rather than followers, and have dominant personalities.

They tend to be focused on specific goals, experience a wealth of creative new ideas, and have the ability to implement these ideas with efficiency and determination. They tend to be courageous and sometimes aggressive. As unique, creative individuals, they tend to resent authority and are sometimes stubborn, proud, and impatient.

(http://www.urbandictionary.com/define.php? term=demitrius)

Why am I telling you all this? Well, it's because all the above was and is part of my personality today. Just as *Jesus* means salvation, so *Hezekiah* means strength to me. I think those characteristics describe me well. The name also bears pain for me because I was named after my father, the *Beast*.

JUNIOR

I was born Hezekiah Morris Jr., the son of a 17-year-old mother and named after my dad who was 23 years old at my birth. I choose to call him the *Beast*, but my thoughts of him changed later in life, and his name changed back to my father.

I didn't ask to be born, and at times thought that my birth was an *accident* of sorts. I had no say-so or control over the circumstances that surrounded my birth and the conditions in my environment. My mom knew nothing about raising children. She was just a child herself. The man she married, my father (the Beast) was an immature person. Because of their inability to raise children, like many struggling parents in that day, my early years were spent with Grandma Morris.

In my heart, I loved my grandmother dearly, just as I loved my mom. She was the mother of the *Beast*, my paternal grandmother. She raised 15 children through her lifetime and saw six of them die at an early age. Her whole life revolved around feeding, clothing, and giving shelter to her offspring, and her children's children. However, and like many mothers back in the day, she barely had time to supervise the children because she was so busy supporting them. Although from the "outside looking in," it all looks good when most kids grow up like that, they raise themselves and grow up on the streets.

BIG MAMA

Grandma was the epitome of a strong Christian woman with a courageous and loving spirit. I guess you could call her "Big Mama." She kept the family together and taught my mom how to be a woman, how to cook, clean, and most important of all, how to raise me, the best she could. My grandmother raised my dad as best as she could, with hopes that he would do the right thing. However, despite grandma's efforts to raise my dad right, he still got momma pregnant at an early age and had a second child with her three years later.

We eventually moved from grandmas into our own mobile home. That's when the circumstances of my childhood began to get worse.

FIRST IMPRESSIONS OF GOD

Like most families living in the southern religious culture, we went to church every time the church doors opened. However, the strange thing that impressed me about God from my church experience seemed to paint a picture of Him as some kind of "Ogre." I understand God as a mean and cruel, unforgiving God, somewhere off in the blue. I didn't have a godly fear of Him, but I was afraid of Him because I thought He would punish me every time I did something wrong.

I began to despise God increasingly. The more I went to church, the more I disliked Him. I was like that because I saw a significant contradiction between Sunday morning in church and the reality of life in the real world where we lived. I thought *what kind of God is He to shout and praise Him on Sunday morning, and yet when I go home, that same God allows my mom to get the hell beat out of her by the Beast. Why would a good God allow my father to become the Beast—a drunken, drug using, abusive man who would beat us uncontrollably?* Therefore, God and I did not see-to-eye.

Don't get me wrong, the Beast was a provider of material things. Unfortunately, some men then felt that if they were providing for their families, that gave them the right to do whatever they wanted, even cheating on their wives', and treating them any kind of way.

21

He worked hard, paid the bills, but he drank heavily and used drugs daily. He was the epitome of the *Temptations* song, *"Papa was a rolling stone, and wherever he laid his head was his home …"*

He was a womanizer, and I guess, "The apple doesn't fall too far from the tree," because I became a Beast too. So, growing up for me was not "good times," it was tough times.

CHAPTER 2

TOO FAST TOO SOON

I was the darkest, or shall I say the "blackest" child on my mother's side of the family. I felt like the "black sheep" of the family, and you know the black sheep is always the outcast.

I was called "black" a lot, so I took the title as a badge of honor. Although it had negative connotations, I used it as a means of becoming a bad person. I had to fend for myself and take responsibility at an early age. I started growing up too fast. When all the attention of parents focuses on just providing, supervision is lost, and kids must manage their own lives.

LAUNCHING OUT

My mother seemed to be closer to my little brother than she was to me, and in some ways looked at me as a man too soon. Perhaps it was because he was the baby boy? Regardless, it left me feeling as if I had to take care of myself.

I liked being away from the house because it made me feel like a man. The Beast would also take me with him to his rendezvous with other women, so I was learning to be a womanizer at a very young tender age. It was fun too!

I met my aunts, cousins, and his other girlfriends, who would give me the attention that I didn't get from my mom at home. My dad and I bonded through those activities, and I loved tagging along with him.

The Funky 80s'

It was the funky 80s,' and funk music was the sound and rhythm of the day. Artist like *Rick James, Earth, Wind, and Fire, Bootsie,* Kool *and the Gang,* and *Michael Jackson,* were taking the country by storm. Bell-bottom pants were in, and Afro's were making way from Gerry curls. We were buying up *curly kits* and wearing stonewashed jeans. It was a "what's happening" time, and everybody felt "Bad," that is good. It was fun times!

We would go to house parties, and the music was bumping "off-the-wall," cocaine was visible, and marijuana was everywhere.

There I was, a vulnerable little boy during grown folk activities, but enjoying it as if I was an adult. They seemed to like me being there too. As I danced in front of them, they would call out my name and laugh as I "cut up" on the dance floor. All of it made me feel like a grown man! I was on "cloud nine" and never wanted to come down. Because I didn't want that feeling to leave, I started chasing it into adulthood. I didn't want the party feeling to ever leave, so I clung to it. It made me feel like I didn't want to go back home.

Flash Back

I started kindergarten when I was only four years old. I was a little black boy with a gap in my teeth as wide as a picket fence. I was afraid to go to school because I had never been away from home for extended periods of time, except for excursions with my dad. I refused to go for the first two weeks.

I cried uncontrollably at the sight of that big yellow bus. I thought it would take me away to jail or somewhere where I would be away from mom, dad, and my family. I believed that it would take me away to a faraway land and leave me

24

there. Those fears and phobias kept me from getting on that bus until grandma used some friendly persuasion.

One morning the bus pulled up, and a teenage girl stepped out of the bus. She had to be at least sixteen or seventeen. Remember, adults influenced me from a young age, and although I was a little boy, I couldn't take my eyes off her. Was I lusting at a young age, or was I mesmerized and infatuated by her beauty? Nonetheless, I have never forgotten that day, and I replay in my mind at times today.

BOY OR MAN?

Her hair was straight, silky, and "jet-black." Her skin was like brown sugar. Her eyes were brown with a mix of coconut color. Her lips were full and plump as a plumb. They glistened like juicy lip-gloss, and her body wasn't like a teenager's body, but more like a woman. Her "hour-glass" figure had me hypnotized. My beady little eyes were fixated on her beauty. I can see her in my mind just as clear as I saw her then!

She approached me, bent down, and wiped the tears from my eyes. Wow, it was like a dream come true! She then picked me up, kissed me on the cheek, and carried me on the bus. My tears dried up, and my frown turned into a smile. I was in love! From that moment on, I didn't want to miss the bus again. My curiosity led me back to the bus repeatedly. Nonetheless, it had a debilitating effect on my life because it led to chasing women.

MOMMA NO!

There was a man in our trailer park neighborhood that we called "Mr. Fix It." He would often come over to our trailer to fix things, but I think he was "fixing" my mom too. One day, I saw him and my mom kissing. Although it wasn't right, I knew it wasn't my imagination playing tricks on me.

The code of silence was in effect, and I was afraid to say anything for fear of punishment.

BEING BLACK!

I was the only black kid in my classes through my early school years. I didn't have a personal issue with race, but in those days, race did become a big problem. We were the generation that transitioned the race issues from the fifties and sixties.

I had a white friend when I was in the second grade. We spent time together, and his mom and dad would take us to this place called *Showbiz Pizza Place*. We would play kid games, eat pizza, and sing along with the band until we got tired. It was so much fun and relief from home.

Every Saturday I was pumped and ready to go with my white friend. That is until one Saturday when they didn't show up to take me with them. I looked at my mom with tears rolling down my cheek and asked her why my friend did not come to pick me up. She replied, *"Your friend's dad called your father, the Beast, a 'boy."*

I didn't understand what all that meant regarding race, so I cried and was angry at the Beast. Once again, he was making life miserable for me and taking something away from me that I liked. All over a stupid name like a boy. Boy meant boy to me and had nothing to do with race.

I didn't know that to be black and to be called a "boy," by a white man, was a bad thing. I didn't know they were saying that we were less than them and worse, less than human. Now I was experiencing my personal Civil War, and I was becoming an angry black man.

CHAPTER 3

GROWING PAINS!

I got over the Showbiz Pizza thing eventually, but my household living situation didn't get any better. Now my dad was drinking more than ever. My mom was more emotionally and physically abused than ever before.

Now older, we wanted to stop him from abusing our mother, but he was too strong for us. The Beast would react and unload his wrath on us with a backhand that would knock us to the floor and send blood streaming from our nose and mouth. We felt like a boxer that had been beaten up in the ring!

Although it sounds like I had already reached manhood, I was only a 5-6-year-old kid. I was at the impressionable age where my learning skills and behavior was still peaking.

BROKEN MOMMA

It seemed like my dad abused my mom and beat her every day. My brother and I were aroused from our beds in the middle of the night, just to look at a woman who was once beautiful, but now she looked like someone getting old before her time. The Beast was supposed to be our protector and haven, but how could he protect us while destroying our mother. My mom was going down fast, and so was I because I couldn't understand why this was happening and why God allowed it.

***

We went from family member to family member to escape the madness of the Beast and living at home. Just imagine the toll that all of this took on two little boys. I was at the age and stage where I needed love and nurture. Instead, I was unloved and tortured. Where was God in all this? I was learning to hate myself and learning to dislike being black. My sense of self-worth and dignity was going down.

I was angry with my mom for not fighting back. I was mad at my family for not intervening and stopping the Beast. I was mad at my teachers for not noticing the hurt and pain on my face and manifest in my behavior. I was learning at a very young age to vent all my problems through anger and hate, which led to doing the wrong things.

The people around my circumstances were programming me to be the man I never wanted to be — a man like the Beast. It is not an excuse, but we can become a product of our environment. Although they were not aware of it, everything and everyone around me was telling me that it was okay to be wrong and do bad things.

PASSING FAST

My life became a self-fulfilling prophecy. I was internalizing the negative words that were being railed at me. Although I didn't really want to, I was becoming like what they were saying about me. (*"As a man thinks in his heart, so is he."*) I would never amount to anything.

Year after year passed and bad words after bad words — *look at you "Blackie" with your pug nose and buckwheat face. Look, it's Zeke the freak. Just look at those dirty shoes and dirty clothes.*

The words of the Beast yelling at my mother, calling her a whore, slut, a bitch nobody, resonated in my young heart. Layer upon layer of what I would become was building on my tender conscience.

My negative self-image began to dominate my personality. I was becoming an ugly, worthless, unloved nobody. That's when I started to put up walls on the inside to protect me from the pain of damaging ridicule of people. What made it even worse was that I didn't feel like my father loved me. I had a great *father wound* deep in my soul. Neither did I feel like my mother loved me. That added insult to injury! She kept my brother close to her and snug in her arms, but it was as if I didn't exist. I thought that the reason was that she looked at me the way she looked at the Beast. I was feeling rejected and just wanted someone to love me "as is."

EMBARRASSED BY THE BEAST

With all the drama and trauma going on in my life, it didn't make life any better when I was in the fifth grade. During that time, the Beast lost his job because the company he worked for decided to move overseas. Unbelievably, the drinking increased, the abuse grew, and stress filled our household. My mom had no job experience, so finances dwindled, and abject poverty was setting in.

There was hardly any food in the house. It seemed like all our money was going towards keeping a roof over our heads. Our clothes were hand-me-down and compared to others we looked like we were poor. I remember eating potted meat sandwiches, cereal with water, or powdered milk. Sometimes all we had was soup to eat for the entire week.

My dad would often escape his responsibility and would leave for extended periods, so it left my mom to fend for herself and us.

The "good news" was that the millwork industry was booming, so my mom got a job as a sewing machine operator. She worked at a place in town called Courtland Mfg. My mom really was a talented woman, and she became one of the best seamstresses they had.

***

One of my most embarrassing moments was when after class one day, my fifth-grade teacher; Mrs. Gregory kept me after school. To my surprise, she filled my book bag and another bag with food. Although I should have felt good to get needed food, I felt the opposite. I felt like a welfare charity case. Besides, I had to carry those bags from the class to the bus, then home. What would the other kids think?

I was feeling so ashamed of my life. I was angry, becoming more hateful, embarrassed, hopeless, and lost. I started crying and asking God why me.

To this very day, I never found out how Mrs. Gregory knew we had no food in the house. I never asked and didn't want to know, but maybe it was God providing at a critical time in my life?

***

I continued to feel rejected and abandoned. I was developing a rebellious juvenile delinquent character. No one could see what was happening to me on the inside because I put up defensive walls all around me.

I started hanging out with the wrong crowd. I became talkative in class to get the attention I wanted and became the class clown. I remember when we had a school play in sixth grade. I was a "ham," so I won the starring role as a raccoon. I knew I could make everyone laugh because my life was like a raccoon.

Art Imitates Life ... I would run around the stage stealing stuff just like a raccoon. I was acting crazy, and the audience loved it and applauded loudly. I loved the attention. I was the focus of attention, and from that moment on, I strove to be the center of attention. However, it was only a mask. Deep on the inside, I felt empty.

I got involved with sports just to get away from home and the Beast. Baseball, football, basketball was an escape.

By the time, I entered Junior High School, my hormones had changed. My sexual drive and other urges were "kicking" in. Now I was about to encounter a significant shift in my life. How would it affect me with such a low self-image?

CHAPTER 4

CLUELESS?

By the time I entered middle school my self-image seemed to improve. However, my self-image depended on my achievements and not on who I was as a person.

I would push myself, and I excelled academically with the help of some good teachers, who exercised patience with me because they saw my potential. I did just enough to get by, and my teachers knew that I had more to give.

I also excelled in sports. Nevertheless, my athletic ability and love for sports declined because my father wasn't there to see how good his son was or to encourage me to perform well. My mother was my main supporter. She took me to my track meets, basketball games, and football games.

LIKE FATHER, LIKE SON

The Beast was still indulging in his three favorite sins: women, alcohol, and drugs, and not necessarily in that order. Those things weren't just his hobbies, they were his life, and as I grew older, his lifestyle affected my way of life. Many ways, I became like my dad.

As I grew into puberty, my hormones surged. One day I stumbled upon my dad's porn collection and my uncle's porn magazines. I thought to myself *jackpot,* and instantly I was addicted. With every chance, I had, I would masturbate.

Because I was shy and girls didn't seem to like me, I focused my attention on pleasuring myself by masturbation.

Sometimes mom would catch me, and I would be punished with a "belt spanking" across my butt. I didn't understand why because I thought it was perfectly natural to masturbate. Nevertheless, the punishment didn't stop me because I was addicted. Pleasuring myself gave me a sense of control, the euphoria of lust, and the fantasy of the women that I desired. It felt like I was involved with the women that aroused me. I continue to struggle with that addition until this very day, but God is delivering me.

EIGHTH GRADE HOODLUM

When I entered the eighth grade, I started hanging out with my cousins and spending less time at home. Hanging out with them, I learned how to smoke cigarettes, drink alcohol, and even how to drive a car. Of course, learning how to drive was not a privilege, but something we did illegally. I was only twelve years old!

We would regularly drive down to the old country store down the road and buy cases of beer and cigarettes. We would then drink and smoke all day long. I loved being away from home because on the streets and around the crowd that taught me all my vices, I felt accepted, and wanted. I was away from the chaos of my home but didn't realize that I was in for far worse problems.

NO STOPPING!

Somehow, the word got back to the Beast that I was smoking and drinking at my cousin's house. Surprisingly, he tried to put a stop to it with verbal reprimands. I guess a father will still attempt to be a father even when he is not setting the right example. Nevertheless, my mother backed her words with discipline, but I continued to go to my cousin's house.

My principal during the close of the eighth grade was Mr. Leverne Marshall. He had a motto that stuck with me through the years: "I am somebody."

Mr. Marshall was a big black debonair man who came from Fayetteville, North Carolina. He played high school basketball with Michael Jordan, and neither was Mr. Marshall was no slouch at the game. Occasionally, Mr. Marshall would show up in gym class and play some pickup basketball games with us. He had amazing skills! Besides being my complexion, what I admired about him most was his discipline and authority. He had a successful life, and he was somebody. He was the epitome of the kind of man I wanted to see in my home!

WHERE IS MY ROLE MODEL?

Thanks to Mr. Marshall, my outlook was changing the proper image of a man. It gave me renewed hope and aspiration that I could be somebody. I now think that God had heard my silent private prayers.

On one occasion, Mr. Marshall and I would pass by each other in the hall, and he would graciously speak to me. I felt like that wasn't anything special, just something he did with every student. Then one day my name was called on the intercom, to come to the office. My heart raced because I just knew I was in trouble! However, I was pleasantly surprised.

When I arrived at the office, Mr. Marshall looked at me and asked me point blank,

"What do you want to be when you grow up?"

I looked at him straight in the eyes and said,

"A Lawyer!"

Mr. Marshall told me that I could be anything I wanted to be, especially if I worked hard. It's funny how life takes

34

you on a twist of fate. Instead of becoming a lawyer, I became the defendant on the other side of the law. However, the story changed, as I get older.

Mr. Marshall handed me a permission slip for my mother to sign. He said that he was taking seven students from our school to Longwood College, which is in Farmville, Virginia. He stated that he picked me because he thought I was going to be somebody.

I experience an array of emotions from excitement to encouragement, acceptance, and support! I finally felt like my life would change for the better. I also felt like my popularity among my peers would get better with that announcement over the intercom and posted notices throughout the school.

I had mixed emotions too because of the comparisons between Mr. Marshall and the Beast at home. Mr. Marshall showed me discipline and authority, but the Beast showed me vices that can be fun. In one way, I wanted both. I needed the Beast because he was my father, but I needed direction and guidance that Mr. Marshall gave me. Whom would I choose and what direction would I take?

***

I needed a better self-image. It seemed like my self-image was elevated, but would it last. I wanted a better life than I had. I needed to be motivated and inspired, but most of all I needed to feel loved and not rejected. I felt rejected at home, so I wanted to get away. The tour of this college campus would inspire and amaze me!

CHAPTER 5

THE DEATH OF THE BEAST!

The buildings were massive, and the atmosphere of Longwood College was impressive. What I liked the most were the cafeteria and the good food. In the cafeteria, they had a variety of foods to choose from—from American to Italian. Yes, sir, I thought, *this was the place for me*.

On the way, back home I quickly made up my mind that I would attend college and become a lawyer. I then quickly filled out my four-year schedule for my upcoming high school years. I arranged all advanced courses so that I could graduate with an advanced diploma. My plans were made, and I had everything all laid out before me. I thought that my success was inevitable. I would do it on my own without my families help. Then came the summer when all my plans would go into effect.

LOSER?

I felt like I was growing into manhood, too soon. I should have been maturing in the areas of learning better social/life skills and how to cope with my problems, but instead, I was suffering from trying to fit in with my peers.

I hadn't even reached the standard of puberty, but I was living beyond my years. My life at home wasn't getting any better either. My depression and loneliness began to turn into anger, bitterness, and frustration. I resented the other kids because they came from respectable families. I hated myself because I was short, black, skinny, gap-toothed, and wore big binocular glasses. I hated God for allowing me to be an ugly duckling with a dysfunctional family. I felt like I was destined to lose at life. I was comparing myself to others and felt like everyone else was better than I was and happy.

TRAGEDY!

Suddenly something happened and changed how I was feeling.

My dad had an accident at work. His leg fell into a hole full of hot iron, and it almost burned the lower part of his leg completely off. He was bedridden for months. While he was recovering, I decided to take over the responsibilities of the man of the house, and I thought I could make things better while he was out of the picture. I figured I was in control.

My time and energy were spent manipulating situations around me and focusing on my new image of a man. However, I covered up the truth and started lying about little things. I was stealing from stores, throwing temper tantrums around the house, cursing, and slamming doors to keep the image of what I thought was a man. Little did I realize that I was just like my dad. Once again, I was becoming a little Beast, and the real Beast couldn't do anything about it.

My mother took most of my lashing out and insults because she was the weak link. It's so true that we hurt the ones we love the most because we re-direct our problems to them. I felt like she didn't love me like she loved my little brother. Besides, she gave me too much responsibility for my age. It was always, *do this, do that, you cannot have this, or you cannot have that.* On the other hand, whatever my brother asked for, he received. I resented him for that!

HATING MY BROTHER!

I remember when it was my brother's birthday, and he was having a "sleep over." All his friend's and a couple of my friends were there. I compared his birthday to my birthday a few months earlier and my birthday was nowhere near the level of his birthday. I didn't get a "sleep over," I didn't get a party, and my gift was a small CD player.

At his party, when he opened the gifts, my mother surprised him with an enormous nicely wrapped gift. My eyes opened wide, and I was envious. My curiosity was aroused at the kind of gift he would receive. What could be in that big box? My brother opened the gift from my mother, and it was a huge CD player. His gift made CD player look like a toy. Instantly I jumped up and went off out of anger. My heart was filled with hurt and humiliation.

The Beast, in the other room, heard my anger and rage and arose from his sleep. With anger in his eyes, the Beast grabbed his crutches, left the room, and came straight for me. Everyone stopped what they were doing. They were all afraid and didn't know what the Beast was about to do. The house got quiet as a mouse. My attention was on the Beast to stop him from doing whatever he was going to do. I felt like in his condition, I had a chance to beat him off me. Today I was going to stand up for myself and not take it anymore. I was going to win, once, and for all.

THE BEAST CHANGES!

My courage was building with each tear that flowed from my eyes. The rage and the anger inside me had my heart pounding uncontrollably. My adrenalin was giving me energy and strength. All the times he cursed us and hit my mother was playing in my mind. The football and basketball games that he missed energized me too. Why he never told me that he loved me was raging in my spirit. All those thoughts fueled my anger.

As he got closer to me, my mother cried out hysterically,

"Please don't!"

He ignored her and focused his attention on me. He then lunged at me with one crutch. It was over his head so he could strike me. I caught the crutch with my hand and jerked it from him. It was like an MMA battle, and I was the champion.

There was a look of shock on everyone's faces and disbelief in their eyes. A father and his small son were fighting! They could only imagine that the man would win and hurt the little boy badly. What will happen next and did they want to see it?

I opened the front door and flung the crutch out of the house as far as I could across the yard. I then turned back to look at him, with my pain and hurt reflected in my eyes, I said,

"You get it…"

At that moment, I became the conqueror that overcame the Beast! The Beast was helpless and stunned, and like a wounded animal walked away. **That was the day the Beast died in my father, and it forever changed him and me.** Ironically, I became the new Beast. That day was a changing of the guard in the home, and I was beginning to take charge.

A New Beast — Bad Ass Me!

Night after night, I would cry myself to sleep. I would say *I would never be like that man*. I promised myself I was going to be better than he was. I was going to say no to drugs and alcohol, but I was going to make the world a better place and everyone would be proud of me. I thought that I would become successful, but inside of me, something else was happening.

In my heart darkness, hate, anger, and despair were growing. I was changing for the worst while my dad, the old Beast, was going in a new direction toward God. He stopped drinking and went to church on a regular basis. I could not believe it! I thought it was too late for God to save him. Where was God when I needed Him and called Him? How could God do that for him and not for me?

I prayed to God all those nights when my mother was being abused, and the abuse persisted. Where was God when I longed for His presence and intervention to save my brother and me from the hands of my father? How could God change this man and not the family?

***

I was still a little boy, and from that moment on, I pulled away from the family values and began to make my own way in life.

I was always smart, so I could handle my schoolwork, but I needed to become a man now. I had to change my image and people's perception of me. I exchanged the glasses for contacts. I swapped my mom's self-made wardrobe for my cousin's hand me downs — Polo, Guess, and Nautica gear. I started going to the barbershop and getting the popular bald fade. I was all most there but what I needed was a bad boy reputation. I needed to be the "dude" who was well known and hung with the cool guys.

I gained my reputation through my cousin. She dated all the top drug dealers in school. They were older, and since they dated my cousin, they would look out for me. I became the friend of drug dealers, and they still respect me today, thanks to Terrell.

***

My family was well known in the city, thanks to my dad, the old Beast. Therefore, my reputation grew even bigger, and I became well known. I was developing a thug life — the new Beast.

CHAPTER 6

MADE IN THE IMAGE OF THE BEAST?

I t was the beginning of my junior year in school. I felt compelled to go to the post office and was surprised to discover an acceptance letter from Emory and Henry College in Emory, Virginia. They wanted me to take a tour of their school and offered me an academic scholarship upon passing my SAT and graduation from high school. On top of that good news, I received five more scholarships from different colleges in a month's time.

However, the image from my past that I was trying to escape was trying to re-claim my life. I was trying to grab hold of God but was losing my grip. I was a lost child that needed something good to happen. I knew God was reaching out to me, but, like many, I was afraid to let go of my past for fear of losing a fun life. Hopelessness started to seep back in!

REPUTATION

I was fortunate to have a job, a car, a girlfriend who graduated from school, money, and a reputation to uphold. School or college was not on my radar, besides who would pay all the expenses for college. My parents didn't have any money, and I felt embarrassed to even tell them that I was accepted to college. That was an odd feeling because children should be happy to tell their parents about their accomplishments. I thought that it would not work out, and I would be a laughingstock. The joke would have been on me.

I had always dreamed of going to college someday. My Grandma Morris and I would watch the battle of the bands, and the step shows from the Historically Black Colleges on BET when I was younger. I would imagine I was there stepping to the music with them, and my grandma would just smile and say, *you will get there one day*. I would hum right along with her. From that moment on, I decided that I would go to college when I graduated. However, I was too busy having fun to think of college then, because sin felt good. My mind was drifting away from that which was best for me. I was becoming "street-wise "and not school smart.

Peer pressure was getting the best of me. As an impressionable teenager, I was hanging out all the time on the streets. I sought my friend's approval and acceptance to give me self-worth. It didn't matter what I got involved in if I was accepted. People on the street whom I thought was my friend gave me the attention I wanted.

THE EYES OF A CHILD

I was often drinking after work. It was the way I coped with my home life, which was deteriorating rapidly. My dad was becoming a believer, and ironically, it pushed my parents farther apart. Mom had been through years of abuse and depended on the Beast, but just couldn't come to grips with my dad being a changed man. She was skeptical, and wasn't falling for the new him, so she starting to pull away from him and the family. She was losing patience with my bad behavior as a teenage boy. I was disobedient, loud-mouth, and just didn't have a care in the world. My lifestyle didn't help the situation. We all needed help, and I was becoming a product of my environment.

One day after school, my mom took me to Grandma Morris's house so she could talk to me about my behavior. She was the only one I would listen to. I remember that day clearly. My grandmother set me close to her and took my hand in hers. She said,

"You know you are my favorite grandson."

"I love you without a doubt, God loves you, and I didn't raise you to be like this."

"You can be better than people around you. You can do better than your mom and dad."

"You are a smart boy. Why don't you use the 'sense' God gave you and make me proud?"

Then she hugged me as if I was a toddler. With tears in her eyes, it was as if she could see the disappoint in my eyes. It was as if she saw all my fear, hurt, and rejection. She heard my cry for help and my yearning for love and affection. She saw in my eyes a child whose parents had failed him. However, what she saw in my teary eyes most was a child who just needed love.

We cried together that day and hugged one another. She kissed me on my cheek and said: *"I love you, and God loves you too."* I looked up at her and hugged her tighter, and didn't want to let go. I then said, *"I love you too grandma,"* as tears started flowing down my cheeks. I didn't know at the time, but this would be the last time I would see my grandma. Whenever I think of her today, Psalm 23 comes to mind because she instilled those words in my heart.

After that day, I decided to do my best to become a better person. Unfortunately, it meant that I would stay away from home as much as possible.

BAD HABITS

I had a job, which I was barely keeping because I was missing work because of my party lifestyle. I also had my car, but developed a new habit, using marijuana.

One evening, I became acquainted with marijuana at a friend's house. We were just sitting around "chit-chatting" about anything that came to our mind. However, when the conversation came to the subject of the girl I was seeing, I discovered he was seeing the same girl. It broke my heart, and I could feel hurt and anger. The pain was only temporary because I had the same harmful experiences at home.

My friend took a cigar out, lit it, and passed it to me. I took it without thinking twice because it stood for manhood to me. I took a puff, inhaled, and exhaled. I was feeling like a man! While we were smoking the cigar, it was as if the weight of the world fell off my shoulders. I felt calm, cool, and collected. I was feeling good! I was a 16-year-old kid who thought he was on top of the world. I didn't realize it then, but it was the marijuana making me feel euphoric. With the mix of alcohol and marijuana, I became the life of the party.

FEELING MYSELF!

I was no longer shy. The way I felt about my looks changed for the better. I wasn't that ugly gap- tooth person anymore. I was "the man." I thought I had arrived and the only thing missing was a girl on my arm. All my friends had girls on their arms, so I thought why not me. The lack of a girlfriend in my arms was solved quickly, because like my father, having a woman around was not a problem.

How I felt about my looks prevented me from sexual encounters, but my first sexual encounter with a girl was at the age of 15. I was timid at first, but after seeing my *boy's* in action, I figured out that I had the same power, and that was money, drugs, and a car.

I wasn't afraid to approach a young woman anymore. My "game" improved, and the words came naturally. I would say things like,

Excuse me miss, but I just happened to notice your beauty from across the room. I'm not trying to step on anyone's toes by any means, but let me know if we can exchange numbers so I can explain to you how I plan on keeping a smile on your beautiful face.

I thought I was Don Juan, and it brings a smile to my face even now because it worked. I was a *"Mack"* (getting the women) and becoming sexually active. For me, sex was a way of control. If I could please a woman in bed, I could make her do whatever I wanted. All the porn that I watched helped too as I tried to mimic porn stars. I was having sex so often with different women that sex became a bad habit, and I was chasing woman just for sex.

"FREAKY ZEKEY"

My friends started calling me "Freaky Zekey," or Zeke the Freak, because of the stories I would tell them. They were stories about all kinds of sex with all sorts of women. I didn't care if she was ugly, fat, skinny, or beautiful. It was all about the sex. They were my prey and victims of Freaky Zekey's world. I may not have been the best-looking guy, but I sure was going to be the best at sex.

At the age of sixteen, my addiction to sex, that I inherited from the Beast, was coming full circle. Back then, the more women you had sex with, your popularity, and reputation would spread in school, and you became "the man." I now had "swag." I was cool, and I had a crew too.

We were known as the Concord boys. We dressed flashy and "fly." We had cars, drugs, the girls, and everybody else's girl. We walked through school as if our "shit" didn't stink. That's how we thought — that we could get away with anything. Girls would flock to us, and the guys at

46

school would hate us. All they could say was, *"There go them, Concord boys."* Our "click" was very close except for one guy. He would always go behind our backs and have sex with our girlfriends. Crazy, but it didn't matter because we were so close, we always brought him back into the crew. The old saying is, *keep your friends close and your enemies closer*.

Aside from working and hanging out with my crew, life was good, so I thought. I wasn't home much and if I was working my parents didn't bother me.

My employment was working at a fast food restaurant, and I enjoyed working there. I was the cook, and on occasion, I would fry all the chicken for that day. I took pride in being able to do a certain job and do it to the best of my abilities.

At the age of sixteen, I was working more than the allotted hours for a teenager. Nevertheless, I liked the times that I worked because it put money in my pocket for the things I needed and wanted. I wanted the best of everything! I thought it was a luxury not to have any bills and no responsibility. Nobody taught me about saving, investing for college, or how to manage my money, so I wasted every penny I got. The money that I was making was going out of the window to support my false image.

CHAPTER 7

THUG LIFE

I started hanging out with my cousin again because she had moved back home from Richmond, Virginia. During that time, I was getting deeper involved in street life, or should I say "Thug Life."

My cousin and I would travel to Richmond about every other day. It was only an hour and a half away from where we lived. When I was growing up, Richmond was labeled the fifth most notorious murder capital in the United States. Because we frequented it so often, it felt like my cousin never left Richmond.

My cousin went to school with R&B sensation, D 'Angelo. He tried to date her, but she turned him down. That's her story. We were watching the Grammys three months later, and he was the opening act and sang "Brown Sugar." I looked at my cousin and couldn't help but think that she thought that the song was about her. Then I just shook my head.

The reason that we were traveling to Richmond so often was because her male friend and future father of her kids lived there. He was a big guy who stood 6'4 and weighed about 270 lbs. He was big black and notorious! He followed no one's rules and was a drug dealer. He was a major football player who played against the likes of Allen Iverson, Dre Bly, and other notable high school athletes from that area. We just called him Black.

STREET-WISE PUNK

While hanging out on the street, my reputation went to another level. I became overconfident, self-centered, arrogant, and narcissistic. I was "hard-nosed" and ruthless. My reputation was sharply increasing. I was finally getting respect on the streets. The streets were showing me the love that I wanted and never received at home. I had all the women I wanted, drugs, and money. I was living the thug life!

I was hanging out with people in Richmond who were deep in the drug game and they associated with some of the top rappers. It was as if I was becoming a celebrity.

Back then, rap wasn't as superficial as it is today — it told a story of life on the streets. It made me feel like I was part of their story. Rappers lived a "hard-knock" life, and they poetically described it in rhyme. The chunky gold chains were in vogue then, and the Timberland boots. We learned about the streets from the likes of Tupac, Biggie, Jay-Z, Nas, Trick Daddy, Outkast, DMX, AZ, and Scarface.

The music then featured DJ Clue, and Ron G. Since we were also close to DC, *Go-Go*, was also influencing our culture. That time in my life, I turned from what was an ordinary country boy life to a city slicker and entered an illegal forbidden realm. I wasn't "hustling," but I was enjoying a hustler's life.

ESCAPE

My street life took me away from all the loneliness, despair, and rejection that I felt at home. I was changing, but not in the right way. I thought I was somebody that my teacher said I would be, but I was another me. I was making a name for myself, and I didn't care if it was becoming another person. Then something strange happened in my life. Satan showed up and destroyed the world I was living in.

My first catastrophe happened when my cousin, and I was leaving Richmond. I was driving my maternal grandmother's car. A sawed-off shotgun, bottles of Mad Dog wine, and marijuana was stashed in the car. We were all underage at the time, and the gun carried a 20-year jail sentence. As we drove out of Richmond, my cousin's male friend, Black, lit the blunt, and we passed it around. Suddenly, we saw flashing lights in our rearview mirror.

We started to panic. Black threw the blunt out of the window and hid the wine, then covered the shotgun with our jackets. I started praying! I had never been near or close to a police officer before, so this was my first encounter with the law, and it wouldn't be my last. I pulled the car over to the side of the road, and the police officer pulled up behind me. He walked towards the car, and my eyes started tearing up because I thought I was in big trouble and I might end up in prison. Images began flashing in my head, pictures of the Beast choking me, then my mom. I saw the wrong of the life that I was living. Then I saw my Grandma Morris and the disappointment in her eyes.

I regained my composure as the officer knocked on the window and motioned for me to roll it down. As I rolled the window down, marijuana smoke blew out of the window. I kept saying to myself we are going to jail. The officer said, *"License and registration please."* I handed the license and registration to him, and he walked back to his car and called it in. A short time later, he walked back to the car and said,

"Sir the reason why I stopped you was because you were going 55 in a 35-mph zone."

I calmly said,

"I'm sorry I was just following the flow of traffic, and I am from out of town, so I didn't know."

The officer looked at me and said,

"Slow it down. There is a police convention tonight so, you didn't know it, but you were following two policemen. So, I'm not going to charge you. You're are free to go ..."

In retrospect, I think God showed up because of Grandma Morris's prayers. When it was over, everyone became silent, at least for the next five minutes. Then Black said,

"Oh, shit we made it out of that one man."

"Zeke, you was smooth with that one."

Black lit another blunt and popped the top on the wine as we continued on our journey home. We never told anyone about that ordeal.

ABANDONED!

It was about a week later when I came home from work. I turned the key in the doorknob, opened the door, and looked in the house before I went in. To my surprise and shock, all the furniture was gone. I ran to the laundry room, and the washer and dryer were missing. My mom and brother were also gone! Then my dad walked through the door, and said, *"It's just you and me now son."* Tears streamed down my face, and I ran to my room. Anger was welling up in me as I thought why! How could a mother abandon her son! How could she leave me with the Beast! How could she choose between my brother and me! I thought *I'm the one who loves you ... I need you, please come back, save me. I'm sorry for being a bad child.* My heart sank. I felt lost, betrayed, like a failure, shameful, guilty, and most of all rejected and abandoned.

The one person that I needed most was now gone. I learned then that beneath the surface, I was a momma's boy, but now my mom was gone! My heart was shattered into tiny pieces, and even today, I'm still trying to put those pieces back together. I still shed tears thinking about when

51

she left me. Again, God was not there when I needed him most.

I never saw that coming into my life. I wasn't home enough to see it coming.

The pain that I was feeling was intense. I started blaming myself for my mom and dad's separation. I then turned to binge drinking to drown my sorrow and medicate my pain. On top of that, I started smoking marijuana every day, all day long. The thoughts in my head were anger towards my dad for all my suffering. I didn't understand why my mother would leave me.

My emotions were fragile, so I turned to the streets for support and answers, and looked to my female friend for help.

CHAPTER 8

WAKE UP!

I t was a rainy night as I was leaving my friend's house. I drank two "forties" (ounces) of malt liquor. I thought I was Superman, so that was nothing for me to consume. I didn't feel any ill effects.

As I was driving in the rain, I hit a water puddle and lost control of my car. Fortunately, the car skidded over to the side of the road and rolled over, and ended up lying on the passenger side. So, I did not get hurt. Was God watching over me again through grandma's prayers? The police arrived, and the officer asked me if I had been drinking. I lied at first, and then he said if I tell the truth I could go home with my father, who had just arrived on the scene. I eventually said yes, I had been drinking, and he released me to my dad.

REGRETTING BIRTH!

The following day I thought my life had come crashing down, but I didn't realize that God was trying to send me a wake-up call. I had no car, no way to work, my mom, brother was gone, and school was starting in three weeks. All I could do was start "cussing" the life that God gave me.

I couldn't turn to God because I was afraid of Him. I didn't want Him to punish me anymore. I thought that God was mean and vengeful and would punish you if you didn't live a perfect life. I certainly wasn't living according to what I thought the standards were, so there was no need to ask God for help.

Casual Acquaintance

I decided to take this downtime in my life to focus on my home life and to get closer to my new female friend.

My girl and I were high school friends and rode the school bus together. We had just become re-acquainted. She also worked at McDonald's, and I would occasionally see her there. A week after I wrecked my car, she crashed her car on the same road, so that event seemed to bring us closer together.

We joked and laughed together, but the relationship went nowhere. I assumed she was dating another guy and wasn't interested in me.

During that summer, the guy she dated ended up getting locked up. We then extended the relationship to talking on the phone. Sometimes we would talk until one of us fell asleep — all night. We would tell each other everything. We then became an item, but our dating was low profile. I was ecstatic because I just "bagged" a winner!

She had almond shaped hazel eyes, high cheekbones, and caramel skin, smooth as silk. She was sexy and beautiful. All the guys at school wanted to get with her. Freaky Zekey was back and had won over the other guys.

We were always talking about what we were going to do after high school and what kind of life we wanted. She was my first love and meant the world to me during that time.

On the first day of our senior year, she picked me up from my house in her new white Ford Escort GT. As I stepped into the car, I looked over at her, and I thought to myself, *I am the man*. I couldn't wait to get to school to show everyone who was on my arm. I was still struggling with my old image because I needed to be the center of attention.

We finally arrived at school, walked in together, and heads turned our way. I was *grinning* from ear-to-ear thinking this is going to be my year. After high school, we drifted in different directions.

GOING DOWN

The reality of my senior year was nothing like I thought. I thought I would be college bound, but I drifted from my ambition and wasn't proud of it.

This was my last year of high school, and I was supposed to be preparing myself for the future. Instead, I treated school like an amusement park. I barely attended, and when I did, I was high. While in school, I hardly did my work. My life was not going upward, but it was spiraling downward.

My high school principal called my family in for a meeting. He wanted to see what my problem was. Of course, the weight of the problem shifted from matters of the home to my behavior. When we left school that day, my anger, and bitterness towards my parents escalated. I was telling myself I was worthless, and broken beyond repair. Therefore, it didn't really matter where my life went from there.

***

During the year, my mom would move in and out of our house only when it was suitable for her. It affected my mental state because my home life was very unstable. I slide deeper and deeper into a dark hole of hopelessness.

Still a teenager, I turned to my own way of dealing with life through self-medicating. I thought I was doing okay by my standards because life had no meaning or purpose for me. My girlfriend left me because I wouldn't stop smoking marijuana. I didn't care because I didn't want to be emotionally close to anyone anyway. My mom moved back out again and my dad who had become a "Holy Roller," was always talking about God this and God that. Unbelievably, I was getting farther away from God too!

**

The only highlights of my senior year were my date with two of the hottest twin girls in the school. I took them to the prom. After the dance, my second-period teacher had me kicked out of his class for the rest of the year because he was jealous of me for taking the twins to the prom. I thought he was a pervert and wanted the twins for himself, so I rubbed it in his face by repeating, *"How great the prom was!"* He seemed to hate that and quickly dismissed me from class. I found out later that he was fired for having an affair with a female student.

GRADUATION

Graduation came, and I still didn't know what I wanted to do with my life, so I did nothing, at least for the first two weeks. That is, all except party and indulge in worldly pleasures. It was all about money, drugs, and sex.

I quit my job and to support my habit, I was selling *weed* ("marijuana") like a full-time job. I had no clue about what I wanted to do with my life and had no idea what the future held. I was young and dumb, fearful of moving forward, and had no direction. Then one day unexpectedly, my friend asked me to ride with him to the Navy Recruiter's Officer. I had nothing else to do at the time, so I said okay.

While he was in the office, I sat in the car. I was finishing smoking a *blunt* that we were smoking on the way to the recruiter's office. While seated in the car I got restless. I started to wonder why it was taking him so long. The temperature outside was above a hundred degrees. I was hot and sweaty, and it felt like I was about to have a heatstroke. Maybe it was the marijuana playing with my mind.

Nevertheless, I decided to go to the recruiters' office to see what was taking so long.

When I walked through the door, the recruiter asked me my name. Then he said,

"You are just the person I am looking for…"

"Do you mind taking a quick test?"

I said,

"Sure, why not …"

I just knew that I would fail the test because I was *sky high*. I took the test and gave it back to the recruiter, then waited for my results. To my surprise and chagrin, I passed the test! Only one of us was going to the military … me. God does work in mysterious ways. Of all people, I was going to the United States Navy.

The way I saw things were that my life wasn't amounting to anything, anyway, so why not. I was stubborn, and on a path of destruction, so I thought that was a workable solution and choice for a *train-wrecked* life. Was God intervening, saving me from destruction?

As we went through the formalities, the recruiter explained to me that I would start Boot Camp in the fall. He also told me that I would be on waivers because of my marijuana usage. To me, it meant that I had the whole summer to have fun.

CHAPTER 9

LIFE WITHOUT GRANDMA

When I arrived home, I told my dad the good news of my recruitment, he was overjoyed! I wasn't sure if he was overjoyed because of me doing something positive with my life or happy just to get me out of the house. Either way, he told me I didn't need a job then because I was going to the military. I didn't care about not having to work. I was thinking that it was going to be a non-stop, never-ending party throughout the summer.

***

The phone rang, and my dad picked it up. It was a call from the hospital, and they informed my dad that his mom, my grandmother (Grandma Morris) was admitted to the hospital. It felt like my heart stopped. Sadness filled my soul. The happiness that I was feeling about the summer all went away like it was sucked up by a vacuum.

My pain for my grandmother was excruciating, and I questioned God again, why? I thought *does God care about me … why is He so angry with me*? My grandmother loved to sing "Precious Lord," so why did He take her from me! I still had so much to tell her about Hezekiah. I was headed to the military, and I wanted her to be proud of her grandson, but now that would not happen.

With a heavy heart, I made my way to the hospital to see her. As I was entering her room, my aunt stopped me and said,

"Don't go in there, she's resting."

I struggled with that at first and was going to force my way into the room, but then respected her wishes. I said,

"Ok, tell Grandma Morris I love her, and I will be back later to see her."

Those were my last words to my grandmother, and I don't know if they got to her. She died later that evening, and I didn't get to see her before she passed. That left a hole in my soul. My dear grandmother was gone! What would I do? When she died, it felt like I died too! I was left in the world alone.

With the help of my editor/publisher, I have composed a poem to my grandmother to let the world know how I felt about her and for closure in my heart.

— ODE TO GRANDMA MORRIS —

My grandmother was my rock and my strength, the only person who would catch me when it seemed like I was about to sink.

She was the only person in the world who was there through thick and thin, who would always bring me back in.

She was always there for me in the eyes of everyone to see that Hezekiah wasn't as bad as he was portrayed to be.

She was there through the bad times, the good times, there all the time.

She was there through the abuses and all my poor excuses.

When I felt lonely and alone, she would always make me feel at home.

When it felt like life had abandoned me, she opened my eyes to make me see.

She made a boy who felt like he was an ugly duckling feel like a handsome prince, even without a kiss.

When I felt ashamed and disappointed, she was there at that moment.

When I made mistakes, she was there to make my case.

She would wipe away my tears and let me know I have many more years to be the man I was made to be, a man, not a Beast that the world would hate to see.

She consoled my soul, and said everything would be all right and hang in there because God would make it right!

I was angry with my aunt because she didn't let me say my goodbyes. We haven't seen or talked to each since my grandmother passed, but as God continues to restore Hezekiah, I believe He will also restore my broken relationships.

THE HAND THAT RAISED ME

I can't explain the love I had for Grandma Morris. She raised me as her child. She poured out love to me like no other, and it felt like it came straight from the heart of God. The values she instilled in me were permanent. I may appear one way on the outside, but on the inside, I am the person she raised.

Grandma Morris showed me how to be compassionate to others through God's *Agape* love. She raised me to be well mannered, polite, sweet, spiritual, kind, always filled with joy, smart, and to be unwavering in my faith. Today, I reflect her heart and soul. To this very day what she transferred from her heart and soul is still in me. She lives through my memories and the character she instilled in me. If was Christ at work through Grandma Morris that is making me a better man; so, my journey continues in the pursuit of Christ to finish the work He started through my grandmother. Christ never leaves us or forsakes us! Grandma raised me to be a godly man, but the journey of my transformation continues.

CHAPTER 10

THE DEPARTURE

The funeral came and passed, and it was time for my departure to the Navy.

I was hanging out with one of my friends one day at a friend's house. We were smoking marijuana and drinking beer. Some females called us and asked us to come and see them. We quickly finished the beer, liquor, and weed, and hurried to meet them.

GOD'S HAND!

While exiting the house, it started drizzling rain. We didn't care about the weather because we were high. As we were driving along with the music blasting, suddenly, out of nowhere a land cruiser pulled out in front of us. There was a loud screech followed by a big boom sound. At that moment, all I saw was darkness as my body was thrown towards the windshield. My head hit the windshield, and a flash of light appeared. Then out of nowhere, an arm grabbed me and pulled me back into the seat, and I blacked out. My door swung open. I could hear voices saying, *"Are you okay."* I could also hear voices screaming and hollering, *"Oh my goodness, his head is bleeding."* They pulled me from the car and laid me on the ground.

The ambulance rushed me to the hospital. The doctor and nurses examined me and said that I needed to see the plastic surgeon in the morning because my wound required healing. I was scared because I did not want to see my face. My mom finally arrived at the hospital as they finished examining me.

As we were driving home, I looked in the mirror and saw my head wrapped in bandages. I sat in the seat and prepared myself for what would be in store for me. An appointment was made for me to see the plastic surgeon the next day.

I got plenty of rest that night and 8:00 a.m. came early. I had been drinking, smoking, and taking lots of pain medicine, so I was feeling no pain.

We arrived at the plastic surgeons. He took the bandages off and showed me the injury in the mirror. He then told me that I wouldn't need a skin graft and that he was going to pull the glass out of my injury and that it would heal over time. That news gave me some relief.

When I returned home, and my friend, who was driving the car, called me to talk about the accident. I thanked him for pulling me back into my seat because if he hadn't, I would have gone through the windshield. I said,

"That could have been fatal."

He replied,

"I didn't pull you back."

"The airbag had me trapped, and there isn't any passenger side airbag in my car."

The first thing that came to my mind was that God stretched out His Hand and saved me! The arm of God and the scar on my forehead is a constant reminder of His presence over me, despite me. When I think of that traumatic moment in my life, Psalms 46:10 comes to mind. *"He says, 'Be still, and know that I am God; I will be exalted among the nations, I will be exalted in the earth."*

64

Stubbornness is one of the most complicated maladies for me to overcome. I should have learned my lesson then, but I didn't. The next day, I was right back at my bad behavior. I had often heard, "A hard head makes a soft behind." I guess my head would need pounding to soften up.

MILITARY NOTIONS

I was beginning to fear the idea of going into the military. I had never had been away from home for an extended period. Consequently, I thought I would sabotage my condition by intentionally failing the drug test.

It was 9:00 am November 25, 1996. Two military officers stood at my door ready to transport me Richmond, Virginia. I would be starting a new chapter in my life. Nevertheless, I was nervous and afraid of the unknown. Considering that I was a seventeen-year-old teenager, the nerves were legitimate. I hugged my mom and dad and said goodbye with tears flowing down my face. After I had embraced them, I turned around and said to the officers, *"I'm ready,"* and I ventured off to my new life. The officers noticed that I was nervous and afraid.

We flew from Richmond Airport to Detroit to Chicago's O'Hara International Airport. We exited the plane and entered a restaurant so I could eat my final meal as a civilian. Everything I heard seemed to say, get up, get in line; you are now the property of the United States Navy. However, I was thinking about catching a bus back home, but that wasn't happening. Now I felt like I wasn't too big and bad.

***

Hundreds of new recruits entered the bus headed for Great Lakes, Illinois. The destination was boot camp, and the ride was quiet. Maybe everyone was feeling like I was feeling — not wanting to go.

We finally reached our destination, and the place where we arrived looked dark and gloomy. There was tension, fright, and nervousness on everyone's face. No one knew what they were about to face. The only thing we knew was that this place was going to be our home for the next 11 weeks.

We all got into line and walked toward shipping and receiving to get our government issued clothing, and the traditional military haircut. We were about to be broken down to nothing and built up again as proud unemotional American soldiers.

MILITARY HORRORS!

I had three drill sergeants. One was a senior chief officer from Korea, one from my hometown of Lynchburg, Virginia, and the other drill sergeant was from the Virgin Islands. They made it their priority to make my first three weeks a living hell! One can only imagine what military life in boot camp would be for a teenager. It was worse than gym class. There are no familiar faces, no phone, no TV, no car, and everything around you are like a horror movie with a three-headed monster running after you. Not a good feeling!

Like a little boy, I cried, pouted, and I wanted my momma and daddy. The reply that came from the officers was, we are your mom and dad now. I tried rebelling against my peers, but that didn't work. I thought that I needed to get out of this place by any means necessary.

I WANT OUT!

We were awakened at two, and 3 am every morning, and there were open bathrooms and showers that made you feel humiliated and embarrassed. I thought, how disgusting. I had never seen a naked man. The making of the beds had to be a certain way, and so was the folding of clothes. Your shoes had to have a *spit* shine, and you had to march regimental style. I was not adjusting to this new way of life at all. Then, of course, there were all the push-ups and sit-ups. We had to stretch out our arms with shower shoes in each hand as exercise. I was doomed! My recruiter had lied to me. I said to myself, *if I ever get away from this place, I'm going to my recruiter a piece of my mind*.

***

Three weeks had passed, and I was still stuck in boot camp. I thought to myself, *there must be an easier way to get through this*. I saw the biggest men get broken down, crying, and getting shipped home. So, I thought *why not me*.

I asked my drill sergeant if they had received the results from my drug test. He said, *"Sorry you passed."* I couldn't believe it! I had smoked *weed* the day before just to make sure I was going to fail the test. I lost all hope of ever leaving that dreadful place.

BREAKTHROUGH GRADUATION!

My three drill sergeants were as different as night and day. The senior chief sergeant was relaxed but feisty when we did not do the right things. He would get angry when we laughed about his size. He stood right at about 5' tall. The petty officer from Lynchburg was cool and laid back. He very rarely got upset. The other officer, from the Virgin Islands (Who I called Mr. Virgin Islands), was a nightmare. You could not talk to him, look at him, much less breath around him. When he walked through the door, it was "f" this, "f" that, and drop on the "mf" floor. He would work us so hard the walls in our barracks would be sweating with moisture. If you messed up on inspection, he would throw everything that you had folded on the floor. He was hell on two feet!

One day, while our division was at *chow*, two other guys and I were hanging out in the barracks with the officer from Lynchburg. Chow was the word they used for breakfast, lunch, and dinner. We were enjoying our one-on-one time with the officer. He asked me,

"Morris, what do you want to do with your life, because there is nothing in Lynchburg?"

I looked up at him and just shrugged my shoulders,

"Hell, I don't know."

He said,

"Well, stick with this, and you will go places that you have never been before, meet women you never could even imagine meeting."

I must admit, when he mentioned women, he had my attention. However, I was still thinking, about getting out of boot camp or at least finding an easier way to get through it. But, now I was thinking about the pleasures he had mentioned. That's when my breakthrough came. My officer said,

"Morris, how would you like to work with the clean-up crew in this building? Your assignments would be to make sure the whole building is clean, and you will not have to stand to watch at night. You will not be with your division much, and you will be on assignment, so when workweek comes, you will not have to be assigned to a job, since you would already have one. Morris, I think you would be perfect for the job."

I said without hesitation,

"I accept."

When I started my new job the next day, I met with the men who were on the cleaning crew with me. The leader of the team was an older man and would be graduating from boot camp soon. They all seemed nice, and I thought the leader was okay too. Really, I didn't care if I wasn't with my division and having to listen to the rhythmic words as we marched together, and the never-ending exercise.

***

One day another person on the cleaning crew and I were cleaning the building when we came upon a soda machine. We were barred from having any drinks of any kind out of the soda machine until we had been to boot camp for eight weeks. I really wanted one of my favorites, a Yoo-Hoo, so my fellow crew member asked me if I wanted one. He said that it would be okay because nobody would know but him and me. So, we shared the drink and disposed of the can. We finished cleaning that day and went back to our divisions. I was awakened early that morning. *"Morris get up and come into my office right now!"*

Those were not kind words! There on his desk was the empty Yoo-Hoo can. I thought to myself that I was set-up by my fellow crew member, and I was. The officer ripped me to pieces with words that I can't reiterate here. He took me downstairs, turned on the TV, and put in an adult movie in the VCR. He turned up the volume and made me stand outside the door. Then he told me to drop to the ground. He asked me to continue doing push-ups until the movie was over. I don't know how many push-ups I did that day, but I think it was well over three-hundred.

In addition to the punishment, I had been assigned to IT for two days, which was Intensive Training. Now I had to get up at 2:00 am in the morning and walk to the gym and do push-ups, sit-ups, or whatever the instructor wanted us to do. After that, we had to run a mile. It is hard to pass IT, and most people failed the first time. However, I figured out a way to use the punishment to my advantage. The good news is I got to eat breakfast twice in one day — once after IT and then with my division.

69

Eating healthy was a necessity in boot camp, and we ate regularly. Therefore, I took full advantage of the routine but didn't tell anyone that I was eating breakfast twice. They kept me on the cleaning crew, so I ate dinner by myself. Despite the discipline, things seemed like they were getting better.

The end of the fourth week in the eleven-week boot camp came around, and I finally was getting comfortable with boot camp. The exercising and marching were getting easier. The men in my division were bonding, and the drill sergeants were easing up on us as well. Wow, we were being transformed into soldiers.

The weeks flew by and after that came graduation. Seaman recruit Morris was now an official member of the United States Navy. All the sweat and tears had paid off. I had persevered.

***

Graduation came and went along with a quick tour of Chicago that lasted through the day. After that, we were shipped off to our A- school to learn an assigned trade that we signed up, for when we registered.

My A-School training was stationed in Virginia Beach, VA, and my trade was OS operations specialist. This would be my home for the next eleven weeks.

I arrived there that evening and received a tour of the base with the other shipmates. It was a huge base with all the accommodations for training. They had a mess hall, medical office, entertainment square, and a store.

To make the transition from boot camp to civilian life, when you first get to your A-School, you must spend your first two weeks on base. Therefore, I took my time, studying hard because my instructor told my class that whoever has the top four highest grades after the fourth week, would get to pick their orders. It meant that whoever finished at the head of the class could choose wherever they wanted to be stationed in the world! Therefore, I studied intensely.

I was meeting new people, but not all of them were good influences. Some affected that negative self-image that I tried to get away from. I had a reputation as a *cool* guy that I wanted to keep up, but that *cool* man image caused bad guy behavior.

The ATL crew that I hung around with indulged heavily in excessive alcohol. My Cali team always indulged in marijuana and sexual encounters with females. The demons of lust and carnal pleasure were re-awakening, but I thought I had control over them, which made me even more vulnerable.

***

The fourth week came around, and my instructor posted the top four names in my class. Yes, I was number four! I was overjoyed and filled with happy emotions. I accomplished my goal!

The instructor put up four destinations: Florida, San Diego, Norfolk, and Japan. The instructor called my name, and I stood up and said, "*Japan, please.*" He told me that I was now going to Japan, and my orders were the following:

You will be working under a four-star admiral, which is the highest-ranking officer in the Navy. You will not be on a ship but assigned to one. You will be on land most of the time, and you will be stationed in Japan for eight years. Also, since you will be under an admiral, your advancement in rank would be faster than your fellow shipmates.

I was feeling great because I was about to live what I only dreamed about — traveling the world. However, the dream would turn into a nightmare!

***

After the fourth week, my motivation decreased because I felt like I had already accomplished my goal. My alcohol consumption increased, and so did my marijuana use. I knew there could be a random drug test, but it didn't matter to me. I began hanging out late at night, partying the night away, and ignoring my responsibilities.

One day, as I was getting out of class, one of my friends came up to me and asked me if I wanted to take a ride with him to smoke a *joint*. I *"said sure, why not."* As we got to the car, two other men, that I did not know, also came along for the ride.

As we were driving down Virginia Beach Blvd, a white van pulled beside us. I stepped on the gas, and when I looked up, I saw a police cruiser at the exit ahead. I began driving faster to blend with the flow of the traffic. The cruiser was now behind me, and now the police lights were flashing. I pulled over, and the cop in the white van jumped out and said, *"Where is the weed, I smell it and saw you all passing it."*

He asked us to get out of the car and put handcuffs on all of us. Instead of taking us to jail, he escorted us back to a base. It was a terrifying moment for me not knowing what would happen! We were put in the base holding cells, restricted, and then sentenced to thirty days in the brig, which is military jail.

I knew that when we were released from the brig, our armed forces careers would be over. Fortunately, we did not receive a dishonorable discharge.

While in the brig, which is different from civilian jail, we got to interact with other peers through work assignments on a daily basis.

BLAMING GOD AGAIN!

I wasn't a bad person but ended up doing bad things and allowing stupidity to overcome my rational thinking. I was disappointed with myself and blamed God again for the mess in my life. I felt ashamed. I was a failure, a loser, a nobody. The pain and sorrow that I was feeling were overwhelming. I was a good person, a good man, but made poor decisions, so why would God abandon me?

My life in relationship to God always perplexed me, and I tried to rationalize my feelings. I was always trying to fill that void inside of me with the notion that someday it would get better, but that day never came. Consequently, while in the brig, I decided to abandon my Christian faith for the Muslim religion. I thought that switching faith would help me to get back on track but was sorely disappointed later.

During that time, the Navy was experimenting with the Islam religion with their recruits. I studied the Islam religion under the first African-American Muslim chaplain in the military. Years later, he was featured in an article in the USA Today.

I was always a spiritual person. I prayed and felt like I knew God. However, in retrospect, as I look back, all I knew was a hollow religion, but nothing about a personal relationship with Christ. I was conditioned by the saying *that religion is for people who are scared to go to hell, and spirituality is for people who have been to hell*.

The Muslim faith did not stick with me. I have nothing against Muslims, and I applaud their commitment and discipline, but it did not resonate in my spirit. I have lots of Muslims friends, but my Christian faith is my personal choice.

My faith problem was that I was looking for an easy instant way to solve my problems, and if it didn't happen the way I wanted it, I had an issue with God. My problem was disobedience.

I was still searching for my identity and the correct self-image. Eventually, I gave up on God and decided to be an atheist. At that point, whatever religion filled my void would be the religion of my choice.

CHAPTER 11

BACK HOME

My brig time was over, and I was headed back home. I had mixed emotions because I hated myself. As I look back at that moment in my life, I thought it was my biggest regret, because I didn't live my dream. To this day, I still have the emotional scars from my disappointments, failures, and wasted opportunities. What would my life be life if I never took that ride? It still hurts and haunts me to think about it.

I would lie to my family and friends about why I was released early. However, the truth has a way of finding a way. Although the truth hurts, it also heals, and I knew I was in the process of healing from my regrets and disappointments.

DEEPER THUG LIFE!

I was back in my hometown and didn't know what I would do with my life. I was always blessed with a decent job, and I soon found employment. I also re-connected with my old party friends. It seemed like I picked up right where I left off. Immediately, I got back into the greed for money, drugs, alcohol, and women. Once again, my life had become unmanageable, and I was spiraling down the wrong path. However, my lifestyle brought to light the need for protection, so I bought a gun from one of my friends. It was a "Chrome .380 Larson" that reflected like a mirror. It was magnificent! When you would breathe on it, it would fog up, then quickly clear up. It was a beauty! I called it my baby, and it made me feel invincible.

I was living out my fantasies and acting like I didn't have a care in the world. I was working, making decent money, my wardrobe was "fresh" and clean, my supply of marijuana was there, and the women were plentiful. I felt like a rap star on a video. By that time, I was only eighteen years old, but living like a grown man.

PLAYERS PAY THE COST

While at work one day I went to use the bathroom. While I was using the bathroom, I felt this excruciating pain coming out of my penis and noticed some white puss coming out. I didn't know what was going on. It was a harrowing experience, and I was scared! I was too embarrassed to say anything to anyone, so I dismissed it. A day went by, and there was no change. I guess I was hoping that it would go away on its own. I called my mom, and she said that it may be a bladder infection, and she told me to drink more water.

I was still very young and in some ways very naive about life. One day I was hanging out with my friends, and casually mentioned what I was experiencing. They started laughing and said, "*Ahh man, you done gone and got that Willie Bobo.*" I thought *Willie Bobo*, that's an STD, what a female transmits to you through sex. One of my buddies said,

"*Man, you better go get checked ...*"

Another friend said while laughing,

"*Man, they going to stick that big ole q-tip in you ...*"

I was thinking to myself *who gave me this*? At the time, I was *fooling around* with about four women at the same time. I narrowed it down to the one that we were all "doing." The Bible says, that if you play with fire, you'll get burned!

Having sex with the same girl was bad enough, but what made it worse I wasn't using a condom. I figured out who gave me the *Willie Bobo*.

I prayed all the way to the hospital, *Lord, please don't let this be Aids*. Aids were starting to be a real problem in America then and an epidemic in the black community.

At the hospital, they did just what my friends said they would do — stuck me with needles. I had to wait five days for the results, and that I would have to contact all the females, that I had sex with. However, I didn't want a reputation as a *snitch*, so I didn't contact any of them.

I was extremely nervous for the entire week, waiting for the results. I would meet the mailman at the mailbox like a person waiting for a check. The results finally arrived, and it read negative for HIV, but I did have an STD. Nonetheless, I was relieved, and said, *thank you, Jesus*.

LET'S PARTY!

There was a party the same day that I got the good news, so I felt like it was time to celebrate. I had been drinking and smoking marijuana all day with my homies. As nightfall came and the party was near, I decided to drive to the city to pick up some more weed. I was too high to drive, but my *homies* didn't stop me.

As I was driving to the city, I dozed off, then suddenly snapped out of it, but it was too late. I panicked and over corrected my turn, and the car flipped over. I thought, *here I go again. Was this a Groundhog Day — Deja Vue?*

When I got out of the overturned car, a woman who witnessed the wreck, came over to help me. She sat me down and made sure I was okay and then left. The State Police arrived and gave me a field sobriety test. I failed the test, then I was handcuffed and taken to jail. Fortunately, I did not have the gun on me, so he only charged me with a DWI, then released me into the custody of my uncle.

SLOW DOWN BEAST!

My car was gone, but that did not slow me down. Apparently, I didn't learn anything from all my earlier mishaps. I was young and foolish.

My dad decided that my brother and I was becoming a bit too much to handle. He had become a Christian man, and I don't think he wanted to face the constant drama that we were creating, so he left. But he didn't leave us empty-handed, so he gave us the house, and moved to the city. What a huge mistake, because now we had a place of our own to have fun all day. An eighteen-year-old and a fifteen-year-old, with their own house, and no parents to supervise? Seriously! That's a recipe for disaster.

***

I distinctly remember it was Super Bowl Sunday. My best friend came to the house to borrow my gun. He had an altercation with someone over a female. I gave him the gun without question.

It was a chilly night, and I was waiting for my girlfriend to call, but my brother was on the phone. In those days, we didn't have call waiting. I was anxious, so I asked him if I could use the phone, but he didn't respond, ignored me, and kept talking. Then my friend returned and gave me my gun, and I put it back under my mattress in my bedroom. My best friend and I talked for a few minutes, then he left to go home.

My brother was still on the phone. Unbelievable! I was furious and walked over to him and *jerked* the phone from him, and hung it up. He reacted by running down the hallway towards my bedroom. I chased him. He quickly lifted my mattress, grabbed my gun, and tried to point it at me. I wrestled it away from him. He jumped up and said "*I got something for you,*" and took off running next door to my grandma's house. I was upset, so I didn't pay much attention to what he had said.

GOD PUT ME IN JAIL!

I put the gun back under my bed, called my girlfriend, and switched off the lights. I laid down to go to sleep. I turned over in my bed only to see lights beaming through my window. I did not know what was happening, but I knew something was wrong. I got out of bed, opened the front door, and two police officers asked if they could come in. Of course, I let them in.

"Do you have a firearm in the house?"

"No ... why?"

"We received a call from someone who said he was your brother."

"He told us you pointed a gun at him!"

I could not believe what I was hearing. How could my brother lie to them like that! The officers asked,

"Can we search the house?"

"Yeah, why not."

However, I was trying to get them to search my father's old room instead of my room. They searched his room and found nothing, so they started talking to each, then looked at me, and said,

"We are going to search the room where we saw the light coming from."

I then led them to my room and sat on the bed to keep them from looking under the mattress. I suddenly noticed that the bullets for the gun were lying on my dresser. Now I was sweating profusely! The officers told me to get up from where I was sitting. They lifted up the mattress, and they saw the gun.

80

"Oh, what do we have here?"

The other officer picked up the gun, checked it out, and said,

"Why is it cocked and loaded?"

All the air in my body seemed to escape. I never thought about checking the gun when my friend returned it.

"Put your hands behind your back, you are under arrest!"

This was the first time that I was officially arrested and arrested for something I didn't do.

I was fuming! Why did my brother lie on me! At the same time, I was angry with God again, for allowing this mess. As I sat in the booking area, I was wondering to myself, *how could I be so naïve. Why hadn't I noticed that I was making bad choices in my life?* My poor choices led to problems, but I redirected the questions to God because I felt like He was punishing me. The judgemental images that I had of God as a little boy was resurfacing. God put me in jail!

***

Surrounded by concrete, and cold steel, I felt abandoned. I was lonely and isolated, depressed, and frightened. As I stood up to be fingerprinted, anxiety and fear welled up within me.

I was given a bright orange jumpsuit and taken to a holding cell with a small slot to receive my food. In the cells were bunk beds, with no ladders. Inmates were lying on different beds, and some were in the common area playing cards or watching TV. I was scared, nervous, and exhausted. Nevertheless, my fear kept me alert because of the tales' I had heard about jail. The meals were served on trays and were cold and tasteless.

All I heard were bar doors slamming shut and then the lock clicking. When I finally laid down in my bunk, I started to pray. Although I felt like God was punishing me, I wanted

Him to have mercy. I began to realize that being in jail wasn't my problem because I was already living in my own self-made prison of drugs, money, and sex. I thought to myself I just needed to start making right choices, and things would get better. My future was looking bleak, and I desperately needed help!

CHAPTER 12

TIME OUT!

My jail experience lasted a week, but it was an experience that I didn't want to experience again. However, and unfortunately, I would experience it again.

***

My court date arrived, and my mother picked me up from the house, and my brother was with her. I didn't say a word to him, and the ride to the courthouse was quiet. I thought to myself that *I could not wait to be found not guilty.*

We arrived at the courthouse, and when they called my case, they escorted us to the back into the judge's small chamber. The judge read off the gun charge then continued to ask the officers what happened that night. Then the judge asked my brother what happened, and he lied about everything. I was floored! Then it was my turn to share my side of the story. The judge then asked my mother who she believed. It bothered me that the judge was making my mom choose between her sons. Was she on trial like the mother of Moses? It seemed like he was making my mom the judge and jury to put my fate in her hands. Would she choose the older son desperately crying out for love and attention or the younger one who lied? The younger son seemed to be her favorite, so I assumed she would say he was telling the truth.

That moment also reminded me of Jacob and Esau in the Bible. Rebekah had so much more love for Jacob than she did for Esau, but Jacob was the trickster and liar, who manipulated his father to get the birthright that belonged to the older son.

CAN YOU BELIEVE IT?

I felt like Esau because my mother told the judge that she did believe my brother and that he would not have said anything like that if it were not true. I was crushed, and my eyes teared up. I dropped my head, and all the hurt, pain, rejection, shame, worthlessness was felt not only in my mind but in my body too. I felt like I was sick! After that moment, I didn't care what happened in the courtroom.

My mother had rejected me, betrayed me, laid me out to be eaten by vultures who stereotyped me. How could a mother betray her child like that! Tears rolled down my cheeks as the judge charged me with brandishing a firearm — a charge that would still be on my record for the rest of my life.

When we left the courthouse, my relationship with my mother was severed and continued to be non-existent. She failed me, and my heart towards her was bitter, hostile, and filled with anger. I felt ashamed to even call her my mother.

Years later, my brother finally told the truth, but the damage had already been done and was irreparable. I struggle to this very day with forgiving my mom. I know that's what God desires of me, but the pain of rejection stands in the way. I have tried to forgive her, but the pain of my suffering is a block and negatively affected my life. I think I can forgive, but it's difficult to forget. I have often read Psalms 27:10 for inspiration:

> *"Though my father and mother forsake me, the Lord will receive me."*

Nevertheless, I still struggled with forgiving her. That day changed my life, and I felt like a loser more than before. I felt dead inside and hopeless. Nevertheless, I put it behind me and was pressing forward. However, I felt like the weight of the world was on my young eighteen-year-old shoulders, but God was making a man out of me.

THE COCAINE BEAST!

At the tender age of eighteen, I decided to leave home and start a new life in the city. I was my own man now, and I thought I didn't need anyone to help me because I would help myself.

I got a job and started meeting new people. Life was going very well again, but I was still drinking and using marijuana heavily to fill the void.

One of my co-workers asked me if I wanted a "tut." He was talking about cocaine and rubbed his nose to signal what he was talking about. I had never used cocaine before, but I was curious. It wasn't like crack, so I gave it some thought. I had seen movies like Scarface, Superfly, and had an idea what it may be like, so I nodded my shoulders and said: "*yes, why not.*" So, I tried it. What could be worse than my life anyway? From that day forward, that white powder began to consume every aspect of my life.

Cocaine affected my relationships, finances, employment, and, most important, my spirituality. Cocaine was now my father and mother that filled the void that my parents left empty. I was in possession of cocaine most of the time and at all cost. It gave me a false sense of control in the bedroom and extended sex. My reputation as a thug was returning because I was in possession of what others wanted. I never dealt cocaine, I was just a user, and at times over-used. "Coke" kept me alert and up all night. I did not want to sleep for the imaginary fear of missing something great.

I traded one addiction problem for another — cocaine for marijuana. I told myself it was a downer … it stayed in my system too long and created more problems. With cocaine, I could drink like a fish and would not stop drinking until all the alcohol was gone. Females were flocking to me and would do tricks just to get my drugs. I felt powerful!

A NEW LOVE

While continuing with my drug-induced lifestyle, I met a woman, my co-worker. We eventually got close as a couple. I was never in a stable relationship before because of my insecurities. They were all adolescent type relationships.

My new love seemed to be all that I ever wanted in a woman, and she was the total package. She had a beautiful smile and a shapely body with well-endowed body parts. The downside was that she had a reputation of involvement with a lot of men, but the cocaine made me feel like I could change her lifestyle. I did know how to treat women, and I knew what women wanted. They wanted love, affection, time, communication, and most of all to be showered with gifts.

I stopped seeing the other women so that I could focus on this one woman. She "stole" my heart and attention, but I couldn't kick my main girl to the curb — cocaine. I promised to keep my cocaine close to me and never let her go. I would keep my love for cocaine a secret from my new love but would continue sharing her with the gang.

EMPTY WITHOUT GOD!

My girlfriend and I started to get very serious and decided to move in together. I was floating on air, and life felt good. Finally, I was feeling fulfilled, but the fulfillment was void of God's presence! When we moved in together, we left God at the door.

I discovered that my love was infatuation and lust. Soon the superficial feelings began to *wear* off we were faced with the reality of our relationship. Without God in our lives, we were left to our own devices to handle our problems.

Cocaine made me a paranoid schizophrenic. I constantly felt like my love was cheating on me. I was a jealous train wreck coming! She was, however, reverting to her old ways, which fanned the flames of my insecurities. So, I started being unfaithful as payback. Cocaine ruled my decisions and was ruining my life. My drinking and drug use continued to increase.

Sometimes I would go days without sleep. My life was getting very radical and out of control — outbursts of rage, a short fuse, missing work and having blackouts. When I looked in the mirror, I saw my father "The Beast" reincarnated. I always prayed that I would never be like him, but it seemed like fate was making me like him. It looked like, through no choice of my own, from generation to generation, the Beast lived on.

Marriage With Baggage!

The idea that I could hide all my screw-ups to cover up my mess-ups to relieve the aches and pains of my insecurities came with the notion of marriage. So, I asked my love to marry me.

In the middle of the kitchen floor, I proposed to her, and she said "*Yes.*" I was a mere immature 21 years old and about to give myself in marriage without maturity and responsibility, and that for the rest of my life. Therefore, I thought that I had to get all my cheating out of my system before I got married. Cocaine and alcohol were doing the irrational thinking for me, and that idea was confirmed by "so-called" friends. Cocaine does numb the brain.

My fiancé was occupied with planning the wedding, and I was occupying myself with avoiding the destruction of the marriage plans. I was trying to be a good man, staying at home, and helping with the planning of the wedding. I also got the opportunity to meet her family. Nevertheless, the streets and my evil activities were calling me. My cravings and appetite for that lifestyle overwhelmed my common sense. I thought I needed more sex, more women, and more pornography when more wasn't even enough.

***

The wedding was getting closer, and I needed to focus, regroup, and get my priorities in order. I decided again to get rid of some of those bad habits, beginning with women, ceasing to hang out, and cutting back on my alcohol consumption. I didn't mention cocaine because I was already married to the white powder, and couldn't divorce her.

As a way of starting over, I also decided to get a new job. I did not want to work there anymore because I felt like the people at work were getting in our business, gossiping, and plotting our demise. PARANOIA! I thought to change, I had to change individuals and places. That way, my life would improve because of a change in environment.

My soon-to-be wife had planned an extravagant church wedding with bridesmaids, groomsmen — the whole nine yards. I picked some men from my old job as the groomsmen. She already had her bridesmaids. My best man would be my best friend, but he couldn't attend, so I chose someone else. I reluctantly chose my father. We decided that my uncle, the Bishop would marry us and that we would get married at her childhood church.

WEDDING DAY JITTERS!

It was the day before the wedding. I had just gotten home from work and was getting ready to go to the church for the wedding rehearsal. I was home alone, and everyone else was at the church waiting for me. While getting out of my work clothes to change into a more suitable attire, my phone rang. It was a familiar voice, an old *flame*, that I had occasional sex with. She was a former co-worker. She spoke with urgency in her voice and said,

"Don't get married!"

"I heard that your bride recently had sex with a male friend from her job."

"It happened earlier this week."

I became numb with silence. My heart jumped into my throat, and I swallowed hard. I only said,

"Thank you ..."

... and hung up the phone. I was devastated, and my shock turned into anger and rage. I then abruptly called the church and said the wedding was off! In retrospect, it was an impulsive decision.

My thinking was distorted, and my mind was cloudy. I didn't at once believe that the woman who called me just wanted me for herself. It was her way of getting vengeance for using her for sex.

My dad came to the house and gave me a pep talk, and I calmed down. He took me to the church to see my lovely bride. When I entered the church, there was burning anger in my eyes, and I could see hurt and pain in hers. I thought to myself, *God does not want us to get married ... we are not ready.*

***

Wedding day finally arrived. My emotions were high, and I was nervous and scared. When I left the house, I fell on my knees, prayed, and asked God "Please send me a sign."

On the way to church, I wanted to be dropped off a block from the church. That would give me some time to think. It was not what I really wanted to do? Was I ready for marriage with such a chaotic life? I just didn't want to do it just for her, but at the same time, I didn't want to embarrass her.

I arrived at the church and entered the door, and it was a large crowd who came to see us get married. I walked down the aisle and stood face-to-face with her. Tears were streaming down my face, but they were not tears of joy. They were tears of sorrow because I knew that something was wrong. I wasn't right, and neither was she. Our love wasn't real, it was lust, and false expectations because others wanted us together, but I couldn't stop now.

My uncle started reading from 1 Corinthians 13:4-8:

> *Love is patient, love is kind. It does not envy, it does not boast, it is not proud.*
>
> *It does not dishonor others, it is not self-seeking, it is not easily angered, it keeps no record of wrongs.*
>
> *Love does not delight in evil but rejoices with the truth.*
>
> *It always protects, always trusts, always hopes, always perseveres.*
>
> *Love never fails. But where there are prophecies, they will cease; where there are tongues, they will be stilled; where there is knowledge, it will pass away.*

After he had read that, I started crying even more and said to myself, *I'm doomed*! I am nothing like what he just read! Then he said, "You may now kiss the bride."

CHAPTER 13

MARRIED TO MADNESS

Life after marriage was a total disaster! We failed in every way. I was so paranoid that I bought a gun to ease my fears of death and destruction.

One night my wife said she heard someone in the backyard walking around. Days before she heard that sound, the tires on our car was slashed. I thought that it may have been one of my old girlfriend's boyfriends, or an old girlfriend. Either way, I felt more secure with a gun.

While my wife was in the shower, I decided to check the gun for bullets. While I was testing the gun, it misfired and went off! I cried out, "Oh my goodness," and took off running out of the house. I was frantic and didn't know where I was running. I was wasting time thinking the police was behind me. My imagination was running wild, and I thought that I might have shot someone next door. I was out of my mind and didn't know what to do.

I ran around the house and thought to hide the gun, but then decided to bring it back inside the house, and stuffed it under the sofa.

My wife suddenly opened the bathroom door, came out, and said, "What was that noise?" I was silent and in shock because blood started trickling down her chest. I said to myself, *fool, what have you done*! I turned away from her and started running again, saying to myself *her daddy is going to kill me. I've threatened her life. Maybe it would be best if I just went ahead and shot myself before her father does!*

IN THE NICK OF TIME!

Reality moment … at the time when she turned around in the shower, the stray bullet grazed her back and just nicked her skin. I thought about that old cliché that says, "He may not come when you want a Him, but He's always on time." I can attest to that from tons of experiences, but I had another fiasco with my gun!

It happened one day when I decided to get off work early. My neighbor had told me that while I was at work, my wife was running around. I was going to stalk her and catch her in the act. I would be the predator, and she would be the prey. Satan loves to use deception so that he can keep you doing the wrong thing. "Two wrongs don't make a right." I should have approached my wife first before buying into accusations.

When I arrived home, my friend pulled up in his car with a big bottle of liquor. I told him what was going on, went into the house to grab my gun, and we went looking for her.

When we reach her cousin's house, I reached for my pistol and went to talk to her cousin. Her cousin told me,

"I don't know what's going on in yall's marriage, and I don't know where she is."

"But I do know she is messing around with some dude across the street."

Then she pointed her finger towards the man across the street. I got in my van and turned it around towards his house. He was talking to some females. I pointed the gun at him while his back was turned away from me, and pulled the trigger twice, and nothing happened. My friend "put the peddle to the medal" and pulled off. It was a delayed

93

reaction, and the gun went off twice while we were driving away. Thank God for His intervention! There had to be a Guardian Angel over us!

COKED OUT-GOT TO HAVE HER

Needless to say, our marriage was over before it started. It didn't last six months. When we separated, I had a different feeling about life. Life really "sucked," and sucked the life out of me. I wasn't eating or bathing. I was mortally wounded, and the pain of being alone consumed me. I was filled with regret about the abuses that I met along the way and the pain I doled out to others. I was self- destructing at an alarming rate. Even the pastor that I asked to restore our marriage said it was hopeless.

One day, while at work, a casual friend introduced me to a higher strain of cocaine. I always swore to never increase my drug habit with any other types of drugs. To me, it was the epitome of the devil, but I became addicted to that hell for fifteen years.

Strong Cocaine deceived me to feeling like my life was complete. It gave me the euphoria of acceptance and love. Actually, it robbed me of my senses. Like the devil, it came to steal, rob, and kill. It doesn't discriminate, it takes everything you have in life and rips it away from you until you are emotionally bankrupt. You lose all respect, beliefs, and values for yourself and everyone you ever loved. It will force you to lie, cheat, and lose your morality. It leaves you without useful options in life because you must have it at all cost. There is no in between.

***

During all the chaos, I met this beautiful woman who eventually became my daughter's mother. I was at lunch during work and noticed this light skinned woman with high cheekbones, a beautiful face, and a smile to die for. I said to myself, *I had to*

94

have her. My first motives were to get back at my wife for cheating on me by sleeping with her friends.

I wasn't trying to hide my addiction to drugs and alcohol but didn't want anyone to know how bad my drug habit was. I was a functional addict.

I finally got the nerve to introduce myself to the woman who would become my baby's mamma. She was seventeen at the time, and we at once connected. She never knew what she signed up for when she met me.

As we got closer, I decided that I wanted her to be the mother of my child. It was like reverse psychology for me. I was called "Blackie" all my life, and it had an adverse inferiority effect on my self-esteem, so I wanted a child the opposite of what I was labeled. I really thought I was ugly with a huge gap between my teeth. So, I thought by having a kid with a light skinned girl, my child would not have to go through what I went through.

I looked at women purely on the surface based on physical attributes and could care less about their character. Today, I think it had to do with my insecurities.

We went on dates, one after another for a while and then we decided to move in together. For a while, I thought I was sterile because no one was having my baby. In hindsight, that was a blessing. God was with me when I wasn't with Him! Seems like God keeps on blessing me in my worse times. Since then, I've learned that's what grace means — God's unearned, undeserved favor. Nevertheless, my desire came to fruition, and she was with child. I was ecstatic and excited that I was going to be a father, but I didn't let anyone know what I was feeling.

BABY MOMMA DRAMA

One night I was hanging out with a couple of friends, and we were drinking and smoking heavily. I become so drunk that I couldn't see or think straight. One of my friends had an idea to go to a party that night, and I was all in. Then he asked me if I would drive. The idea was to have the whole crew to attract the women.

During the same time, my baby's momma was leaving her cousin's house, and some guys on the block asked her to give them a ride. She was headed their way, so she obliged them and told them to hop in.

We arrived at the party at the same time, but she passed us first, and my friend noticed the men in the car with her. He said, "*Isn't that your baby momma in the car with those dudes?*" I reacted and turned to see what he was talking about. My friends started instigating an altercation, so I felt like I needed to show my manhood, or should I say, my childhood.

When we pulled up to the party house, I got out of my car, walked over to her, and as she was letting down the window, I punched her in the face. She became frantic and got out of the car, trying to explain her situation.

"*Baby, why are you doing this?*

"*I didn't do anything wrong!*"

But I didn't hear it. I was showing out to my boys. I pushed her away, and she fell.

"*Bitch, that baby ain't mine!*"

"*Admit it ...*"

I then turned around and jumped back into my car and speed off. I was filled with unjustifiable rage fueled by marijuana and alcohol. My reality was distorted.

We drove away from the party and hid out in the country away from the police. The next morning my phone rang, and I was humiliated and embarrassed to learn about what I had done. Again, God intervened in my mess and the baby survived.

When she told me the truth about why those men were in the car, I realized like never, that I had to get my mind right and give up the intoxicants.

A week earlier, during a party, a friend asked me,

"What are you going to do with your life? You have it all to be so young. You've been married, traveled from state to state, traveled the world in the military, and owned several cars. When are you going to slow down? If you keep going the way you are going, you are going to lose everything chasing nothing!"

Those words played in my mind like a dagger in the heart. I had to get it together. But, fate seemed to still be my enemy, and I wrecked my car on the way home from another party two weeks later. To add insult to injury, I also got a DWI. A week later I checked myself into a treatment center.

DETOX OR NOT

I told everyone that I was detoxing from my alcoholism, but it was really for my drug addiction. I was no doubt an addict, and I finally learned to acknowledge it. I wanted to do everything I could to get clean, and a treatment center was what I needed at that point in my life. I needed to get away from my negative environment and former friends. I needed to rest and change my focus from the streets.

***

The treatment center gave me the opportunity to detox, in an unfamiliar environment. "Out of sight, out of mind." I could remove the fog from my brain. They gave me snacks and food whenever I was hungry, so proper nutrition became a part of my diet. I wasn't running the streets and had time to evaluate my life. Some good counselors helped me to refocus my life, while I was sober. They helped me to think straight to find a solution for "why." I learned that the problem usually stems from fear-based emotions that I picked up in

97

my childhood. I learned that I was a chronic worrier, filled with anxiety, anger, hostility, rage, ill-will towards others, resentment, frustration, impatience, and irritations.

The treatment center also introduced me to AA and NA programs. AA stands for Alcoholics Anonymous, and NA stood for Narcotics Anonymous. They were 12-Step Programs to help you stay clean and to meet others who were trying to stay clean. We would use little clichés like "You need to have an attitude of gratitude," that would stick in our minds.

When my thirty days of detox was over, I continued to go to the meetings. I stayed clean for a little while after leaving the center but would relapse. Each time I relapsed, I would slide further and further away from the normality of life. I would drink more, do more drugs, and I started stealing to support my habit. My life wasn't getting better, it was getting worse!

CHAPTER 14

DEFINING MOMENTS

There is something special about a child being born into this world! The Bible says in Psalms 127:3-5,

Children are a heritage from the Lord, offspring a reward from him.

Like arrows in the hands of a warrior are children born in one's youth.

Blessed is the man whose quiver is full of them. They will not be put to shame when they contend with their opponents in court.

My daughter was born on February 18th, 2004, and her birth gave me a special feeling that I had to get my life together to better raise my daughter.

It was by far the happiest moment of my life. Holding this helpless child in my arms and knowing, that she was begotten by me and part of my blood line, gave me a new sense of pride. It also gave me a sense of God's unconditional love because we are His children, so if I felt this way about my baby, I could only imagine how God felt about me, made in His image. I said to myself and spoke aloud to my daughter in my arms that I would always protect her. I would always be in her life and love her. I would take care of her, and she would never have to go through what I went through in life. However, "promises are made to be broken."

A BAFFLING ADDICTION

I once heard Larry King say, "We're old enough to stop being ashamed of our father when we have children who are old enough to be ashamed of us." That saying didn't make much sense at first, but when my baby was born, what it really meant came home. It meant that I had to change my life! Nevertheless, my addiction would stifle my responsibilities. My addiction was cunning, baffling, powerful, and compulsive.

Instead of being a father I ruined everything I touched. I was stealing from my family and places of employment to feed my habit. I hit rock bottom and felt like I was in a wilderness. My relapses were more frequent. I was spiritually bankrupt. I was a lost boy.

***

I really don't know how my baby's mamma coped with raising my daughter and putting up with me. Because of that, I have a profound respect for her. She was a blessing throughout the ordeal, and any man would be grateful to have her as his wife. Despite my habit and behavior, she managed while I was out hanging out at the drug house. She was teaching my daughter virtue and values while I was getting worse. I was in and out of treatment centers, while she wiped tears from my little girl's eyes.

While she was putting my daughter's first tooth under her pillow, I was chasing a hot girl, in my view, the hottest in town. While I was running around, my baby's momma was putting my daughter on her first school bus. This strong black woman was both mother and father to our child.

TIME PASSES

101

The years passed on, and I missed being a part of my daughter's life! I eventually lost all hope that I would ever be clean and free of my addiction. My Life had no meaning. Nevertheless, Scripture came to my mind from Romans 7:19-20, *"For I do not do the good I want to do, but the evil I do not want to do—this I keep on doing. Now if I do what I do not want to do, it is no longer I who do it, but it is sin living in me that does it."*

I began to realize that my habit wasn't just an addiction, but it was a sin problem!

My babies momma and I finally had split up, and I didn't blame her one bit — it was all on me.

TO HELL & BACK

I met another woman at the at the Narcotics Anonymous meetings, and we formed a relationship. I was always told never to date anyone from NA because it was like a double-negative. It was all about the sex, but she took me to the depths hell.

We came together to have a drug induced relationship which always ended with me going to jail. We would use whatever drug was available and use it to act out our sexual fantasies. We were deluded to think that we loved each other, but it was a sexual bond, not real love.

She was a habitual liar or a pathological liar. I thought men were the only ones with that disease. I never had a police record until I met her. I'm not blaming her because I had problems before I met her, but my problem was deeper than drugs. Although God intervened at critical times in my life, I was spiritually empty, void of the reality of Christ.

Once, during an alcohol-induced blackout, she called the cops and told them I had assaulted her. Say hello to my first felony! Another incident happened while I was driving her to get some pills. I tried to avoid a sobriety checkpoint, but they caught me, and I was charged with a DWI, and eluding the police. Of course, she lied and said that I did try to dodge them. We were a co-dependency problem!

***

Our relationship was filled with emotional and physical abuse. We carried baggage from past relationships that we took out on each other. As if I had a home life, I struggled to balance home life with my fantasy drug induced world.

I thought that a good life was about having a housewife, a four-bedroom house, a white picket fence, two and a half kids, a car and a van, and a dog and a cat. My reality was far from the truth! Eventually, I moved away from my baby momma and child and back to my hometown. I was trying to start a new life.

IN JAIL, AGAIN

Guilt and shame followed me wherever I went. How do I unload this baggage of my past! Maybe it would work out if I just faced my past demons, so I tried to make the relationship work with my co-dependent addict.

The first time the jokes on you, the second time the jokes on me, but the third time, I am a fool. Within a month of my co-defendant sexual partner moving in with me, the police were visiting us again.

I didn't have the ability or strength to end this toxic relationship. My life was self-destructing right before my eyes, and I felt helpless to do anything about it.

One night I got on my knees and prayed, "Dear Lord, I don't know how, but please release me from Satan's hold." God hears our prayers even when we think He does not.

***

Time went on, and my young family turned their backs on me. My daughter didn't want to have anything to do with me. She implied as a child that the woman that I was with was evil.

103

I had wasted five years of my daughter's formative years, and I could have avoided it all. No one else was in control of my destiny, but me. It was about my bad choices, nor drugs, alcohol, or women. From that moment, I saw that the past ten years, my world revolved around the jail and illegal activities. I was out of place in society as a dysfunctional man. I thought that my fate was to lose at life. I was a product of a broken family and toxic environment.

***

One day I left work upset that my new female companion decided to take a break up with me. Nevertheless, that was okay because there were other women out there, so I called her because I didn't want to feel lonely at that moment.

We started drinking alcohol and playing cards, and I started feeling better. When we ran out of alcohol, I went to get more because I usually drank till I was totally inebriated. Night came, and I was wasted. I had blacked out, and when I woke up, I was in jail without no bond. My past had caught up with me again.

I couldn't believe what took place while I was blacked out! In my drunken stupor, I decided to call a cab to go home, but on the way, I decided to pay a visit to my ex's house. I didn't have cash in my pocket, just a debit card. The cabbie called the police because I couldn't pay with a debit card. The police came and discovered that my "ex" had a restraining order on me, so they arrested me. I was in jail with no bond. Thus, I lost my job, livelihood, and freedom in an instant over a dumb decision. With every decision comes a consequence. Our choices determine our fate.

While I was in jail, I didn't want to talk to my lawyer because I was denied bond, and I thought he didn't try hard enough anyway. I didn't want to hear or talk about God because I thought He didn't listen to my prayers. If He did, why was I always in trouble?

***

My life started flashing right before my eyes like I was dying, and my jail time was a defining moment.

The pain inside of me was intense, and my light of life seemed to fade. The feelings of disgrace and anger were burning on the inside of me, and like flames to a fire, I was burning up. I wanted out of life.

When you are in jail, guards watch your every move, and they make decisions for you. I took those things for granted in the real world and my days in prison were all the same, like Deja Vue.

My lowest moments in my life came whenever I was arrested. Telling my family that I was a felon hurt a lot because I embarrassment them. Those thoughts led to tears of regret. In my mind, those prison bars were not the creation of the system, but my creation. I put myself behind those bars. My life was over!

I was asking myself why and where I went wrong. I was living for the drugs, which robbed me of a good conscience. I thought I was cool, but I was just a fool. I thought to myself that getting older and acting like a hardened criminal — living the thug life — was not what I thought.

CONCLUSION

RESCUED!

David, the bad boy, cried out in Psalms 34:6, *"This poor man called, and the LORD heard him; he saved him out of all his troubles."*

My life was a constant cry out to God, but I thought He didn't hear me. The old folks use to say, "God don't listen to the prayers of sinners," so I figured I had to clean myself up first to become a Christian. However, since then, I have learned that's not true, God hears a sincere prayer that comes from the heart, regardless of who is praying. God doesn't discriminate. I've learned that the real key to getting prayers answered by God has to do with "what" you are praying for. If we are just praying for blessings of material things without our lives changing, then don't expect God to answer that kind of prayers. But if you are praying for salvation as a means of changing your life, then you can expect God to answer that prayer at some point. The problem for most of us is "when."

THE PRICE

Unfortunately, many of us had to pay the price before we came to Christ, but it's nothing compared to the price He paid for us.

I know there is a price to pay for every action because we really do *reap* what we *sow*. But, I have also learned that the opposite is true, anyone can turn their lives around and reverse the sowing and reaping process. That is, we can begin to do good to offset the bad. That does not mean those good works is the answer. It means when we live better, things will get better.

***

My perception of life was wrong or misconstrued. I learned that I was religious but did not have a relationship with Christ. My life was empty and void of meaning because Christ wasn't in my life, just my thoughts. Therefore, I believed that others could "fix" me, instead of looking to Christ.

I thought that everyone was better than me and different from me, but now I know that we are all God's creation and different one from another. These are the thoughts that led to my Restoration — being restored to the image God created in me.

I SAW THE LIGHT!

I believed what people told me about God and me, instead of finding out for myself in the Bible. That false belief system put me on the wrong path in life. People said that I would never amount to anything, and I believed them. Proverbs 23:7, "...For as he thinketh in his heart, so is he."

I believed I was an outcast, a violent force of nature. I believe there was not an honest bone in my body. I felt like I was so close to hell you could smell the fire and see my flesh burning away, but why I wasn't dead. **I was not arrested. I was rescued through my troubles because I became aware that only Christ could help me.** When we are at our wit's end, then God can step in!

***

In jail, I saw my secret prison on the inside of me. I was down in the belly of the beast, and it was dark. It had no walls or bottom, or a way out. I saw a light appear dimly, and I squinted my eyes so I could focus clearly. It started getting brighter and coming towards me. I heard a voice say,

"Hezekiah."

And it repeated itself,

"Hezekiah, where are you, Hezekiah?"

The voice continued,

"I answered your prayers ..."

"I rescued you from many troubles."

"Now you are free!"

My voice trembled, and I stumbled over my words and said in a low tone,

"My Lord!"

Tears began to flood my eyes, and I said,

"Take me, Lord, let your will be done."

"Forgive me Lord of my sins."

"I am sorry I have failed you and my family."

In an instance, I started to move towards the light. My eyes opened wide, and I fell out of my bunk, got on my knees, and prayed to my God,

"Come into my life and be my Lord and Savior!"

I thanked him for His undeserved, unmerited grace. I thanked Him for his mercy for saving a sinner like me. I thought about all the trials and tribulations I had gone through, but they were nothing compared to this defining moment. That day my hope and dignity were restored!

GOD WAS THERE ALL THE TIME

God was there all the time and had never left me. I left Him at the church door. I'm reminded of a poem I once heard.

One night I had a dream.

I dreamed I was walking along the beach
with the Lord.

Across the sky flashed scenes from my life.
For each scene, I noticed two sets of
footprints in the sand,
one belonging to me, and the other to the Lord.

When the last scene of my life flashed before me,
I looked back at the footprints in the sand.
I noticed that many times along the path of my life
there was only one set of footprints.
I also noticed that it happened at the very lowest
and saddest times in my life.

This really bothered me
and I questioned the Lord about it:
"Lord, you said that once I decided to follow you,
you'd walk with me all the way.
But I have noticed that during the most
troublesome times in my life
there is only one set of footprints.
I don't understand why
when I need you most, you would leave me."

The Lord replied:
"My precious child, I love you and would
never leave you.
During your times of trial and suffering,
when you see only one set of footprints, it was then
that I carried you."

by Mary Stevenson

I will remember that experience and encounter for the rest of my life. I will hang the poem up as a constant reminder, where I can always see it, and everyone who visits my house will see it too. That poem is a reflection on my life. That day, in a moment and in the twinkling of an eye, my life changed forever!

I have come to realize in life that we are either in a storm, coming out of a storm, or headed for a storm. But the storms are few and far in between, and the good news comes after the storms. I have had major storms my life, and I know that I will have more, but I will go through them differently because Christ is now in my life.

I know now that I was not looking for love, I was running from love in fear of commitment and real intimacy. It was never about my relationships or sex, it was about my relationship with Christ, that was missing. It was about me acting out of my inadequacies, rage, self-hatred, and the need for control.

BREAKING GENERATIONAL CURSES-THE BEAST IS DEAD

My father (The Old Beast) only knew what he learned from his father, and I knew only what I had learned from him, and we passed it on to our sons and daughters. However, when we come to Christ, that cycle is broken, and it's up to us to follow a new path in life that the Lord lays out for us. It just means that when Christ comes into our lives, we don't have to live like those before us. We now have strength and grace to turn the corner to new directions. It's not magical or mystical, it's simply about obedience to the Lord.

***

I know that the trials that God took me through gave me the strength to endure, and made me stronger. It gave me the strength to choose my friends wisely. I no longer need false friends to be complete, I am complete within me, with Christ in my life. Someone once said, "The biggest room in the world, is the room for improvement." I know that I still have a long way to go, obstacles to overcome, and weaknesses to be made secure, but with Christ, I now know I can.

I don't think that anyone ever reaches a plateau in life where they say, I have arrived. We will always have the demons of our past chasing us and trying to put us back in bondage, but Christ already took care of that on Calvary, so I won't worry about my past catching up with me. The truth is, it's gonna take some time to change.

I realize that I'm still young and my journey is long and is by no means easy, but I am now free to do the right things. John 8:36, *"So if the Son sets you free, you will be free indeed."*

Because of my past, some people will doubt the integrity of my life and think I'm just faking for some reason. That's okay because I know that God doesn't judge me based on my past, He looks at my future, and so do I. In the spirit of meekness and repentance, I will win hearts of the haters and doubters. I know that trust and respect must be earned and by God's grace, I will win it.

Regardless of my past, I can choose my future. The most important part of my life has not been lived yet. I thank God that my worst times in life are behind me, and the best is before me. I have found the goodness of good and will not let it go, and it is in Christ Jesus. His grace sustains me.

We may not experience the freedom from adverse circumstances, bad habits, and evil hobbies when we want, but God's timetable is right on time. **Trust God, and He will make a way out of no Way!**

ABOUT THE AUTHOR

Hezekiah Morris is a 41-year-old alpha male. His leadership skills have been understandable from childhood. He was born in Appomattox Virginia. He now lives in Lynchburg, Virginia.

Hezekiah has known Sherica Lanette from youth and young adulthood, and after meeting again after seventeen years, they are now engaged to be married. Hezekiah has one brother and one child, Kyla Israel.

Despite his trials, Hezekiah graduated Magna Cum Laude from Skyline College in the Computer Engineering Program with a 3.7 GPA and made Dean's list. He is now a Material Handler/Machine Operator with hopes of pursuing a career as an ordained minister, with a concentration in counseling.

Hezekiah enjoys reading, sports, and spending time with his family.

Hezekiah's dream is to enlighten and empower as many troubled youth and adults as possible by sharing his story. He wants everyone to know that anyone can change and that life gets better through faith in Christ.

The most important truth that the reader should be aware of about Hezekiah Morris is that he has a compelling story to tell that can change the lives of young urban dwellers. Hezekiah did not come from privilege but never felt entitled — like the world owed him something. In fact, he felt like he owed those who struggle through life. He tells his story with authenticity, without holding back the truth and telling it in graphic detail.

www.ingramcontent.com/pod-product-compliance
Lightning Source LLC
Chambersburg PA
CBHW020917180626
46816CB00007BA/2451